F   Snyder, Zilpha
Sny   Keatley.
        The diamond war

PERMA-BOUND

AR 3pts
BL 4.4

THE
DIAMOND
WAR

 TIFFANY, 14   KATE, 10
CARSON, 7   FIFI (POODLE)

 BUCKY, 11   MUFFY, 9

 RAFE, 17   GABE, 13   CARLOS, 10
SUSIE, 8   LUMP (SAINT BERNARD)

 LOTS OF GRANDKIDS

 EDDY, 10   WEB, 8

 LAURA, 13
NIJINSKY (COLLIE)

 AURORA, 10   ARI, 8   ATHENA, 4

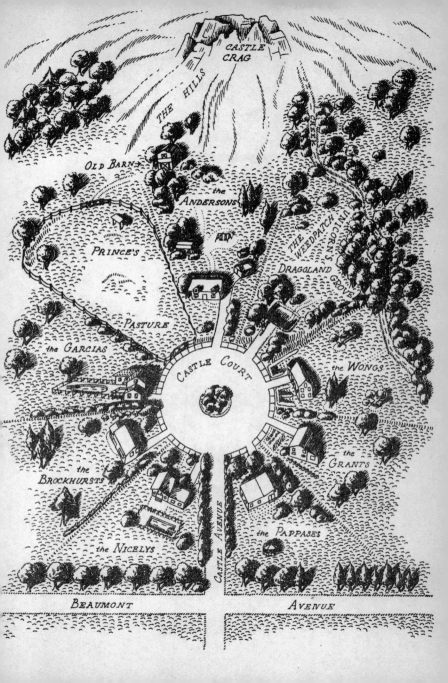

CASTLE COURT KIDS

THE
DIAMOND
WAR

Zilpha Keatley Snyder

A YEARLING BOOK

Published by
Bantam Doubleday Dell Books for Young Readers
a division of
Bantam Doubleday Dell Publishing Group, Inc.
1540 Broadway
New York, New York 10036

ISBN: 0-440-40985-3

Printed in the United States of America
June 1995
OPM   10 9 8 7 6 5 4 3 2 1

For kids and dogs everywhere

Chapter

1

It was early on a Saturday morning and light was just beginning to slant across the cul-de-sac known as Castle Court. Long shadows reached out from each of the seven houses, and a damp fog still drifted under the tall trees that grew on the mysterious vacant lot. In the misty morning light the great jagged crag on the hill above the cul-de-sac looked, more than ever, like an old ruined castle.

The sun was just clearing the hilltops when a back door slammed open at number three Castle Court. Number three was a big new Spanish-style house with a tile roof and an enormous swimming pool, and the person who came out the door was Carlos Garcia.

Carlos was wearing swimming trunks and carrying a Dove bar. He stopped for a moment on the big back deck to look around. Next door, at the Brockhursts', there was no sign of life. The Brockhursts slept late on Saturdays. But on the other side of the Garcias' lot something was moving. Just barely. It was the Andersons' old Shetland pony trudging slowly across his pasture.

Carlos watched the pony absentmindedly as he unwrapped the Dove bar, dropped the wrapper on a bench near the back door, and ran down the steps. But his mind wasn't really on the pony, or on the Dove bar either. And it certainly wasn't on the loud sniffing, slobbering noise that came out from under the deck and then followed him as he crossed the lawn. He knew it was only Lump.

Lump, the Garcias' enormous Saint Bernard, could smell ice cream half a block away. He sniffed and slobbered and whined hopefully as he lurched out from under the deck and followed Carlos and the Dove bar. Carlos was usually a soft touch.

But today Carlos had other things on his mind. He jogged around the swimming pool and out onto the diving board. At the end of the board he lay down on his stomach and went on eating—and thinking.

Lump stood at the other end of the diving board for a minute or two, licking his slobbery lips. Then he sighed loudly, climbed up the stairs, and ate the ice cream wrapper. Carlos didn't notice that either. He was much too busy thinking about his wonderful idea.

Carlos, who was ten years old and in the fifth grade at Beaumont School, was a good athlete, and he was also good at solving problems. Particularly sports problems—like where to put first base. By the time he'd finished the Dove bar he was pretty sure he'd come up with something that just might work.

As soon as the ice cream was all gone he flipped the stick into the water and dove in after it. It was a professional dive, straight and clean. A minute later he climbed out of the pool with the stick in his mouth. He had grabbed the stick in the water like a shark catching a fish. Carlos liked to do tricks like that, even when there was no one around to watch.

On the back porch he stopped long enough to blot himself a few times with a towel before he hurried to the kitchen telephone. He had to call Eddy immediately to tell him about his great idea. Eddy would be really excited.

Eddy Wong, who lived right across the cul-de-sac at number six Castle Court, was Carlos's best friend. Except, of course, for Bucky Brockhurst, who was another kind of best friend. But it was Eddy who was going to be really crazy about Carlos's idea.

The phone rang three times before Eddy's mom answered. She sounded rushed and a little breathless as she said, "Oh, hello, Carlos. I'm fine, thanks.

Yes, I'll call Eddy but he can't talk very long. We're just going out the door. So just a short conversation. Okay?"

"Okay," Carlos said, but what he was thinking was, *Rats*. Eddy had told him they were going to visit relatives today, but he'd forgotten. The Wongs were always visiting relatives in the city.

"Rats," he said out loud. The trouble was, his great idea wasn't going to be easy to explain in a hurry. He'd just have to get to the important point right away. He was reminding himself to get to the point in a hurry, when Eddy picked up the phone.

"Hi, Eddy," he said excitedly. "You know what? There'll be plenty of room if we put it right in the middle of that little forest. I mean, after we chop it all down."

"Yeah?" Eddy said in a questioning tone of voice. Then for a few seconds he didn't say anything. "I don't get it," he said finally. "What are you talking about, Garcia?"

Carlos sighed impatiently. He should have known that jumping to the main point wouldn't work with Eddy. Eddy liked things to be in order. He started over. "It's about having a baseball diamond," he said. "Right here at Castle Court." That would get Eddy's attention.

Eddy was the one who had been wanting a baseball diamond more than anything—and Carlos knew why. Here at home there had never been enough room for a diamond, so Eddy and Bucky and Carlos had played other games. Or game, really. Like, nothing but basketball for years and years and years. And Eddy, who was a great batter and pitcher and all-around good athlete, just happened to be a little bit short.

Short doesn't matter in baseball, but it certainly does in basketball, particularly when you're playing with Bucky Brockhurst. Carlos didn't blame Eddy for being tired of basketball. He himself got a little tired of losing every tip-off and rebound to Bucky— and he was two inches taller than Eddy.

"What baseball diamond?" Eddy said. "Where?"

Carlos knew that would get him. "The Weedpatch," Carlos said. "At Dragoland."

"But there's no room," Eddy said. "Remember? We measured it. If you put home plate near the basement, the creek is in the outfield. And if you go the other way, there's no place for first base."

"I know," Carlos said triumphantly. "That's just it. There will be lots of room for first base if we just chop down—"

"Eddy! Come on. Right now!" It was Mr. Wong's

voice and he sounded like he meant it. Eddy yelled good-bye and hung up the phone.

"Rats," Carlos said again. With Eddy gone he had only one other PRO to talk to—and that was Bucky Brockhurst.

Chapter

2

The PROs were like a special club. A club just for guys who played sports a lot and who were all planning to be "PRO-fessional" athletes when they grew up. Actually there were only three full-time PROs, plus a bunch of part-timers. The part-timers were mostly guys from other neighborhoods, plus a couple of Anderson grandkids. But Anderson grandkids were around only on weekends and holidays. So the only real, original, full-time Castle Court PROs were Carlos Garcia, Eddy Wong, and Bucky Brockhurst.

Carlos sighed. The thing was that even though Bucky was just about the greatest athlete at Beaumont School, and you couldn't help being a little bit proud to be his best friend, he wasn't always all that great in some other ways.

Like, for instance, you never knew what Bucky was going to do. He might be all for Carlos's plan or he might not. It all depended on the mood he was in. He might get all excited and want to start chopping down everything in sight. Or, on the other hand, he might decide he wasn't interested at all. He could even go back to saying what he'd said when Carlos and Eddy first started talking about having a baseball diamond at Castle Court.

"It'll never work," Bucky had said. "The Weedpatch isn't wide enough. And no other place around here is deep enough for a diamond. Not if you have any real sluggers anyway. Like me, for instance. You remember what happened that time we tried to play out in the street, don't you?"

Carlos remembered, all right. He'd pitched the ball and Bucky had batted it right through the Nicely's picture window. "Yeah," Carlos said. "How could I forget? I got my allowance taken away for a month. Playing baseball was Eddy's idea, and you hit the ball, but I was the one who lost my allowance."

"Well, poor old you," Bucky said. "I lost my allowance too."

"No, you didn't. You had lots of money the very next day. Remember all that stuff you bought at my dad's restaurant?"

"Oh, that," Bucky said. "That wasn't my allowance. That was just blackmail money. I was blackmailing Muffy."

"Oh yeah?" Carlos said. He should have guessed. Muffy was Bucky's sister, and the "pay up or I'll tell" routine was something they used on each other a lot.

"Yeah," Bucky said. "But Muffy's getting real sneaky lately. I haven't gotten anything good on her for a long time. So I sure can't afford to lose my allowance. So you better just forget about playing baseball around here. There's just no place big enough for—"

Carlos sighed. "Yeah, I know. There's no place big enough for a slugger like you." He might have gone on to say that Bucky just wanted to keep playing a game where he had a natural-born edge on everybody else. Like, being a lot taller than most people in the fifth grade.

That had been the end of that conversation. So there probably wasn't much use calling Bucky. But with Eddy gone, Bucky was the only real PRO left to talk to. Carlos pretty much had to tell Bucky about his great idea, or nobody. He picked up the phone again and dialed the Brockhursts' number.

Bucky answered the phone on the second ring, and he seemed to be in one of his better moods. He actually seemed to be listening while Carlos explained his idea about how to solve the first-base problem.

"Sounds okay to me," Bucky said. "A lot of work though. Hey! Unless we had a chain saw. That's what we need. A big old chain saw."

"Yeah," Carlos agreed. "A chain saw would be great. But I guess axes and lots of muscle power would do the job."

"Well, maybe," Bucky said. "Your dad got any axes?"

"I don't think so," Carlos said. "You don't need axes very often in a restaurant. How about your dad?"

"Naw. No axes. But he does have a killer hatchet I could use."

"A killer hatchet?" Carlos asked uneasily.

"Yeah. You know. Great, neat, awesome. That is, I can use it if I can sneak it out of the garage without my dad noticing."

"Why? Won't your dad let you borrow it?"

"Not anymore he won't," Bucky said. "Not since I chopped up a bunch of junk when I was practicing making a Boy Scout campfire. It sure looked like a bunch of junk to me, but it turned out to be this expensive antique my mom just bought at a garage sale. Sooo . . . no more hatchet time for the old Buckaroo."

Carlos laughed. That was Bucky for you. Making

a campfire out of an expensive antique sounded just like Bucky Brockhurst.

"Chopping down all that stuff just might make enough room for first base," Bucky said. "But it won't be easy. That's a lot of trees. And I can't help till tomorrow. I got to go to town with my folks this morning. They're going shopping and then we're going to a movie. I don't know when we'll come back. Let's do it tomorrow. Okay?" Then he laughed and made a loud "brrr" noise. "Wish we had a chain saw," he said again. "Brrr!"

Carlos sighed. "Okay, tomorrow," he said. "We'll start tomorrow. Maybe Eddy will be home tomorrow and he can help too." Carlos really wanted Eddy to be there when they started.

It was when Carlos was saying good-bye that he realized he'd been hearing funny noises for a while now. Clicking noises and a loud breathing sound, like somebody was listening in on one of the other phones. But Rafe and Gabe, Carlos's brothers, had gone to the restaurant with his dad, so no one was home except his mom and little sister. His mom wouldn't listen in on someone else's conversation. Of course Susie might—not that it was likely. Susie wouldn't be at all interested in a conversation about baseball diamonds. At least that's what Carlos thought.

After he hung up the phone Carlos headed for his room to change his clothes. It was while he was sitting on the floor pulling on his socks that he happened to notice a sports catalog under his bed, so he scooted over and pulled it out.

The PROs were going to need a lot of new equipment to go with the new baseball diamond. The next thing he knew he'd been sitting on the floor with one sock on for a long time, picking out the balls and mitts and bats they would have to buy. In fact, he got so busy deciding among Rawlings and Cooper and Wilson that he forgot all about the mysterious breathing noise he'd heard on the telephone.

Chapter

3

While Carlos was still sitting on the floor picking out the best catcher's mitt, the front door opened at number one Castle Court and Kate Nicely came out carrying a large paper bag.

Kate, who was in the same fifth-grade class as Carlos, had straight brown hair, fierce blue eyes, and a brown belt in karate. Everybody at Beaumont School knew about Kate's brown belt, just like they knew that Kate Nicely and Aurora Pappas were best friends.

Kate closed the front door carefully with one hand while balancing her paper bag with the other —and stumbled over Nijinsky. Nijinsky was a collie dog who lived across the cul-de-sac with the Grant family. He was on the front porch waiting, as he did every morning, for the Nicelys' poodle to come out and play. Even though Kate had almost fallen on him, Nijinsky, who was a very friendly dog, wagged his beautiful collie tail and put up a paw to shake hands.

"It's no use waiting," Kate said as she shook his paw. "Fifi isn't coming out today. She urped all over the kitchen floor last night and Mom thinks it might be something catching like distemper."

Nijinsky's ears drooped and his forehead wrinkled. "Don't worry," Kate told him. "It's not really distemper. It's just lizard poisoning and I don't think it's fatal." She leaned forward, lifted Nijinksy's drooping ear, and whispered, "She ate one of Carson's favorite lizards last night. But don't tell. No one saw her do it but me."

Kate smiled as she gave Nijinsky a last pat and picked up her paper bag. As she started down the steps she was thinking that talking to animals was another weird habit she'd picked up from Aurora, not to mention the rest of the Pappas family. Weird —but interesting. That was how you'd describe the whole Pappas family, all right—weird but interesting.

A minute later, as Kate was about to knock on it, the front door of number eight Castle Court flew open. A very small girl with a dark corkscrew ponytail flew out and almost ran into her. Athena Pappas was still wearing her pajama bottoms, her T-shirt

14

was on backward, her feet were bare, and she had a big carrot in one hand. She dodged around Kate and slid to a stop.

"Hi," she said breathlessly. "Aurora's waiting for you." Then she waved the carrot and went on running.

"You're late," Kate called after her. "I'll bet Prince is mad at you."

Aurora's little sister, Athena, who was only four years old, was crazy about animals in general, and horses in particular. And even more particularly, Prince, the Andersons' old Shetland pony. Every morning since she was two years old Athena Pappas had insisted on visiting Prince before she would eat her breakfast. In fact, Athena's prebreakfast visits were kind of a neighborhood joke.

Kate grinned, thinking about what would happen if Athena were a Nicely instead of a Pappas. At the Nicelys' nobody did anything until after they'd eaten their breakfast. A proper breakfast with napkins and place mats and gooey oatmeal in the wintertime. Kate was still watching Athena running toward the pony pasture when Aurora came to the door.

Aurora Pappas, who was a month older than Kate Nicely but quite a bit smaller, had Alice-in-Wonderland hair and large cloudy gray eyes. She was wear-

15

ing a backpack over a long paint-smeared T-shirt that hung down almost to her knees. Probably one of her mom's. Aurora's mom, who was an artist, wore paint-smeared T-shirts a lot.

"Hi," Kate said. "You ready?" She pointed to her paper bag. "I've got all my stuff. You got your stuff?"

Aurora nodded slowly. "I think so. And you know what? I think . . ." Her huge cloudy eyes widened and a faint smile flickered across her face. "I really, really think . . ." She paused and her eyes got even wider. "I think *this* will be the day."

"Yeah," Kate said firmly. "I think so too. Let's go."

Kate Nicely and Aurora Pappas walked down the gravel path between the Pappases' two big old cherry trees and turned to the right on the circular sidewalk. When they were almost to the vacant lot that everyone called Dragoland, Aurora smiled and pointed. "Look," she said.

Across the cul-de-sac three little girls were hanging over the fence at the Andersons' pony pasture. The two blond ones were Anderson grandkids. The one with the brown corkscrew ponytail was, of course, Athena. Athena was patting Prince's old head where it hung down low over the fence.

16

"Shhh," Kate said. "Don't let her see us." She grabbed Aurora's T-shirt and pulled her down the narrow path that led back to the Weedpatch. Aurora followed quietly. When they were safely behind a tall bush they stopped and peered out through the thick leaves. Athena was still standing on the bottom rung of the fence.

"Good," Kate said. "She didn't see us. That's a relief."

Aurora nodded. "Yes," she said. "She's really too young to be a unicorn maiden. And besides, she hasn't had her breakfast."

Chapter

4

Not long after Kate and Aurora left the Pappases' house, the door opened again and a small boy with a pointed nose, sharp eyes, and a huge mop of curly hair came out. It was Aurora's eight-year-old brother, Ari. He looked around quickly, ran across the front yard, and climbed up into one of the big old cherry trees. When he was comfortably seated in the crotch of the tree he pulled his fanny pack around to the front, zipped it open, and took out a brand-new notebook. Opening the notebook to the first page, he carefully printed ''THE BIG NEW GARCIA EXPOSÉ STORY by Aristotle U. Pappas.''

Ari, who was in third grade, had been writing in cursive for quite a few months, but he always printed his titles in big dark letters so that they would look like the headlines in a newspaper.

Ari was practicing to be a reporter. The kind of reporter who goes around investigating all sorts of interesting secrets about terribly important people and then writing "exposé" articles about them. Someday the secret things he wrote about would be in newspapers and magazines and even books, and he would become rich and famous. He wouldn't mind signing his books with his real name then. For a kid, having a name like Aristotle was a pain in the neck, but it would be just right for a famous investigative reporter.

So far Ari hadn't met any very important people so he practiced by writing about the people who lived where he did—in Castle Court. None of them were terribly important, but some of them came pretty close. Like the Garcias, for instance.

From where he was sitting in the cherry tree in his front yard, Ari could see part of the Garcias' house. It was a big house. The biggest one in the court. That was because the Garcias were pretty rich. A long time ago Mr. Garcia had been a famous baseball player and now he owned a sort of famous restaurant. So writing about the Garcias was pretty close to writing about famous people. Ari was still trying to decide which one of the almost famous Garcias to practice writing secret stuff about when the front door of the Garcias' house opened and Susie came out.

Susie Garcia came out of the big double front

doors of her house and slammed them both behind her. Hard. Then she started across the circle. If Ari were more like his sister Aurora, he probably would have had a mysterious supernatural feeling that an important story was heading his way. Aurora had mysterious feelings all the time. But the only thing Ari felt at that moment was that Susie was angry. "Wow!" he whispered. "This time she's *really* mad at somebody." He sure hoped the somebody wasn't him.

Susie kept on coming, swinging her fists and glaring. She stomped around the planter island and headed directly toward Ari's house. "Wow!" he said again. He couldn't think of anything he'd done lately that might make anybody that angry. But with Susie you never knew. When she was right under his tree he took a chance and said, "Hey, Susie."

Susie jumped about a foot. Then she looked up and frowned harder than ever. She didn't say anything. Even though Susie Garcia was in Ari's class, third grade at Beaumont School, she never talked to him very much. In fact, at school Susie never talked to any boy if she could help it. At home Susie had nothing but big brothers, so at school she liked to talk to girls. Like Ari's sister, Aurora, for instance. Susie particularly liked talking to Aurora. Susie went on not saying anything so Ari said, "You want to see Aurora?"

"Yeah," Susie said.

Ari put his pencil behind his ear and his reporter's notebook in his teeth. Then he swung down out of the tree. When he was on the ground he took the notebook out of his mouth and said, "Aurora isn't home right now."

Susie glared at Ari. Then she stuck out her lower lip and blew a bunch of curly black bangs off her forehead. "Where is she?" she demanded.

"I don't know," Ari said. "She and Kate went off somewhere."

He really didn't know. Not for sure. Actually, he had a pretty good idea, but he also knew what Aurora and Kate would do to him if he told. Particularly what Kate would do to him. Kate might not be quite as good at mysterious feelings as Aurora, but she was very good at karate. "What did you want to see her about?" Ari asked.

"I've got something to tell her," Susie said. "Something very important."

"Well," Ari said. "She'll probably be home in an hour or two. Could you tell her then?"

Susie sighed angrily. "I don't know. Maybe not. I might not be mad enough by then."

Ari felt his ears prick up. An experienced investigative reporter knew good story material when he heard it. But he didn't take his pencil out from behind his ear and get ready to write. He knew that would be a mistake. Being too interested made people get suspicious and shut up. Instead he just said, "Oh yeah?" in a slightly bored tone of voice.

Susie nodded. "Maybe I'll decide not to rat on him after all." Her eyes narrowed and she stuck out her jaw. "Maybe I'll just go home and . . . and . . . stick a knife in his basketball—or something."

"Oh," Ari said. "Carlos, huh?"

"Yeah," Susie said. "The creep! He ate up all the Dove bars. A whole box full. And they were mine. I bought them with my own birthday money." She frowned at Ari. "How'd you know it was Carlos?"

"Well, Rafe plays football mostly, and Gabe plays the guitar. Carlos is basketball, right?"

Susie shrugged. "Yeah, basketball." But then her eyes narrowed again. "That's just it. That's what I wanted to tell Aurora. Carlos and the rest of those creepy PROs are going to start playing baseball too."

Ari was puzzled. Carlos and his friends, Eddy and Bucky, played basketball all the time. They played in the summertime and in the winter. They even played before breakfast in the morning and after dark in the evening. Sometimes they played in their own driveways and backyards, but mostly they played on the old cement driveway at Dragoland. As far as Ari knew they never played baseball very much because there wasn't enough room for a baseball game anywhere in Castle Court. But what Ari didn't get was what any of that sports stuff had to do with Aurora. He took his pencil out from behind his ear and scratched his head with it. "Yeah?" he said.

"Yeah," Susie said. "And do you know where they're going to put their baseball diamond?"

Ari had no idea.

"At Dragoland," Susie said. "Back in the Weedpatch at the back of the lot. *And* first base is going to be right in the Unicorn's Grove. They're going to chop down the whole grove with Bucky's hatchet."

"Wow!" Ari said. He was surprised—and excited. He was surprised because he didn't know that Susie even knew about the Unicorn's Grove. And he was excited because he had a feeling that he was on the trail of a very important story. He was planning his first sentence when he realized Susie was still there. And still asking questions about where to look for Aurora.

"You might try the barn," Ari said. "They've been there a lot lately."

Susie's frown faded. When Susie wasn't frowning she looked something like a baby rabbit. "What do they do at the barn?" she asked.

"Well, it's some kind of a ghost thing. They do this thing about the barn being haunted by the ghost of some mysterious Anderson ancestor."

"Yeah? Ghosts?" Susie's dark eyes always seemed to shoot sparks when she was really interested.

"I guess I'll try the barn," she said and took off running at top speed. Susie did a lot of things at top speed. Ari sighed. He felt a little guilty about sending Susie off to the Andersons' barn on a wild-goose chase. And it would be a wild-goose chase because he'd investigated enough that morning to be pretty sure that Kate and Aurora were doing the unicorn thing again today. And that was always at one special place.

Ari tucked his pencil and notebook back into his fanny pack and started up the sidewalk. It didn't take long. Just past the Grants' overcrowded flower beds and the Wongs' neat boxy gardens you came to a tangled jungle of trees and bushes, and there you were. In the vacant lot that everyone called Dragoland.

Actually the best thing about the vacant lot was

24

that it wasn't really vacant. A long time ago, when the Anderson family's Castle Farm was just being turned into Castle Court, some people named Dragoman bought lot number five. Then after they'd started to build a very large house they suddenly stopped and went away. They went away leaving a brick foundation around a half-dug basement, an extra-wide cement driveway, an empty fishpond, and a jungle of trees and bushes. At the back of the lot was the big flat weed-grown field known as the Weedpatch.

Nobody knew for sure why the Dragomans went away. There were a lot of rumors. But nobody wanted them to come back. At least none of the kids did.

Everybody played in the vacant lot called Dragoland. Over the years nearly every Castle Court kid had dug clubhouses in the basement, which was known as the Pit. Almost every year there was a new tree house in one of the big old oak trees. Little girls played house or hopscotch in the dry fishpond. The Weedpatch was a great place for small games of soccer or touch football, and the whole place was perfect for hide-and-seek. And, of course, Carlos and the other PROs practically lived on the old cement driveway, which had been made into a basketball court.

And—way at the back of the lot, between the Weedpatch and the creek bed, there was a thicket of bamboo and young acacia trees that was called the Unicorn's Grove. At least that was what it was called by Kate Nicely and Aurora Pappas and a few of their closest friends. Not to mention a certain investigative reporter who knew about a handy spying place in a clump of bamboo at the far edge of the grove.

When Ari reached Dragoland he took the quickest route to the back of the lot, a narrow path that twisted through the jungly vines and bushes, dropped down into the Pit, crossed it, and went up the other side.

Once out onto the Weedpatch he walked quickly and quietly, heading toward the creek bed and a thicket of small trees and bamboo. When he got near the thicket he started to tiptoe.

He was still tiptoeing, going around the trees toward the creek, when he began to hear the music. He grinned. They were there, all right. He stopped, and for a moment he thought of going right on in. He would burst right into the center of the grove and quickly tell them why he'd come. Quickly— before Kate had time to start getting violent—he would tell them exactly what Susie had said *and* what the PROs were planning to do to the Unicorn's Grove.

But then he chickened out. To burst right in, even if he talked very fast, would be just too dangerous because of Kate's karate training. He could talk pretty fast when he had to, but a karate chop was probably even faster. So he went into the grove by his usual route after all, at the back where the bamboo was so thick that only a weasel—or a very skinny eight-year-old reporter—could wiggle through. Could wiggle into the grove on his stomach as he had many times before. Closer and closer, until he could hear everything, and see most of what was going on in the clearing. Resting his chin on his hands he settled down to wait for just the right moment to jump out into the clearing and—very quickly—tell them that he'd come to warn them about a terrible danger to their own private and personal Grove of the Unicorn.

Chapter

5

While Carlos Garcia was still sitting on his bedroom floor picking out a catcher's mitt, and while Ari Pappas was still talking to Susie, important things had been going on in the Unicorn's Grove. Kate and Aurora had been very busy and now they were almost ready. Almost but not quite.

"Ouch," Kate said. "Watch out. You're pinning my ear."

"Oops. Sorry." Aurora pulled on a pin and a paper flower fell off the band she was arranging on Kate's head. Kate's brown hair was straight and slick and her flowery wreath kept sliding down over her eyes. Aurora's wreath—a gray terry-cloth sweatband decorated with pink paper flowers—was already on her head, almost buried in her heavy tangle of crinkly sun-streaked hair.

Aurora picked up the last flower and carefully pinned it back where it belonged. It had to be just right. In the books about unicorns all the maidens had wreaths of flowers in their hair. "There," she said at last. "That looks great. Just don't move your head too much when you dance. You know. Twirl gently. Like this."

Aurora raised her arms and twirled across the tiny clearing in small graceful circles, holding her head very still. Her long hair and her sheer white robe swirled and flowed around her, and her bare feet barely seemed to touch the grass. When she got to the other side she stopped and looked back at Kate. "Okay," she said. "Your turn."

Kate's sheer white robe matched Aurora's because both of them had come from the same room in Kate's house. At Aurora's house no windows had ordinary decorations like sheer white curtains. That was because the Pappases were artistic. At Aurora's house windows had beads or stained glass or even peacock feathers, but never curtains. But in the books the maidens who tamed the unicorns always wore long white robes, so it was lucky that Kate's mother liked white curtains.

Aurora thought Kate looked beautiful in her robe and wreath, even though the wreath kept falling down over her eyes and some of her twirls looked more like karate than ballet. When Kate finished her dance they both sat down under the sacred acacia tree, and Aurora opened her knapsack. The first thing she took out was her unicorn book. She didn't even have to open it to the picture of the maiden taming the unicorn. The book opened there all by itself.

When the book fell open Kate suddenly pointed and said, "Look." She was pointing to the tree in the picture of the unicorn and the maiden. "That's a willow tree, isn't it?"

Aurora nodded. "Yes, a weeping willow."

Kate looked up over their heads. Her forehead wrinkled in a worried frown. "And that's an acacia tree, isn't it? Do you suppose that will make a difference?"

For a moment Aurora's gray eyes clouded, but then she smiled. "I don't think so," she said. "Look, it says this picture was painted in Belgium. So—if our unicorn was Belgian it might make a difference. But a California unicorn probably won't notice." She nodded slowly. "In fact," she said, "a California unicorn might even prefer acacia trees."

The next thing Aurora took out of her knapsack was her Walkman. As soon as she turned it on, unicorn music began to play. It was strange music, high-pitched and wavering, like the sounds of wind and water. Actually it was a tape that belonged to

Aurora's father, who liked to listen to weird things while he was doing his metal sculptures. Aurora and Kate had listened to a lot of music before they picked it out. They both thought it was just what a unicorn would like.

Aurora turned down the volume. Then she took out Kate's silver unicorn. Both Kate and Aurora had unicorn collections at home. They had unicorns made of china and clay and plastic and even spun glass. But Kate's silver one was the most beautiful. And the most powerful. Aurora put the silver unicorn in the middle of the clearing, where its power could spread in all directions.

Next was the golden bowl. Actually the golden bowl was made of brass, but it was the right color. Aurora arranged the bowl carefully on the ground between herself and Kate.

"Now," she whispered. "The water from the crystal fountain."

Kate took a bottle of Perrier out of the knapsack and poured it into the golden bowl. Then she took out the blood-red apple and the magic wand. When the wand and the apple were arranged next to the bowl there was nothing left to do. They sat very still with their legs crossed and their hands resting, palms upward, on their knees—and waited.

31

According to Aurora's book, unicorns liked to eat blood-red apples and drink water from sacred crystal springs. The unicorn would come to the grove because it was hungry and thirsty. When it saw the golden bowl and the maidens in their white robes, it would kneel down beside them. It would drink from the golden bowl and eat the apple. And if it let them touch its beautiful silver horn it would be theirs forever.

Aurora had truly believed in unicorns since she was three years old. She didn't know if she truly believed the unicorn would come to the grove today, but even if it didn't come today she wouldn't stop believing. She didn't know for sure if Kate believed in the unicorn, but she knew that Kate would say she did if anyone asked her. Kate always said she believed the same things Aurora did.

It was very quiet in the Unicorn's Grove. Aurora's legs were beginning to feel stiff and cramped. She straightened them out and then crossed them again. Kate was sitting very still. It was wonderful how long Kate could sit without moving when she really wanted to. When it was important to whatever she and Aurora were doing, Kate could do all sorts of remarkable things. Aurora was still admiring how

Kate was sitting when she began to hear the strange sound.

It was a whispery, shivery noise, like something moving in the dry grass. Perhaps like the sound of a timid unicorn carefully following the smell of a blood-red apple. Aurora started to poke Kate, but it wasn't necessary. Kate had heard it too. Kate's eyes were wide and startled-looking.

The noise started and stopped and started again. Aurora could almost picture dainty unicorn hooves picking their way through the bamboo and acacia saplings. She was still listening and waiting, sitting very still with her open hands on her knees, when she heard another sound. A gasp and then a sneeze. A very definite sneeze.

"Ahh-choo!"

Chapter

6

When Aurora backed out of the bamboo thicket she was dragging something after her by the back of its shirt.

"It's Ari again," she said. The "again" was because Ari was always following people and spying on everything they did. And it certainly wasn't the first time Kate and Aurora had caught him red-handed.

"*Ari!* I told you!" Kate said. What Kate had told Ari was that she was going to use him for karate practice if she ever caught him spying on them again. Now she was poised and ready, her chopping hand flat and stiff. Ari hadn't seen her do it, but he'd heard she could crack a brick with that hand.

"Wait a minute!" Ari squealed. "Wait a minute! Don't chop. It's not my fault. I had to come tell you. I have something very important to tell you."

Kate didn't lower her chopping hand.

"It's a matter of life or death," Ari said frantically.

"I know," Kate said. "Guess who's going to die?"

"It's about the grove," Ari blurted out. "The Unicorn's Grove."

That was a mistake. Kate and Aurora looked at each other. "How'd you know about the Unicorn's Grove?" Aurora asked. "I never told you."

"It doesn't matter who told me." Ari's voice was turning into a desperate wail. "What I have to tell you is that the PROs are planning to chop it down. They're planning to build a baseball diamond right here in the Weedpatch, only it's not wide enough so they're going to chop down the grove. Carlos and Eddy and Bucky are going to chop all this stuff"— Ari gestured around him—"all these little trees and bamboo right flat down and put first base right here. Right here in the middle of the grove."

Aurora caught her breath in a sharp gasp, and Kate's chopping hand came slowly down. They stared at Ari with wide eyes.

For what seemed like a long time no one said anything. Kate was the first one to begin talking—and asking questions.

"When?" she said.

"Tomorrow, I think. Susie said she thought they were going to start tomorrow."

Kate and Aurora looked at each other and nodded. "Susie," they said. "Yes, Susie knows about the grove." Susie Garcia was always trying to be a part of their games. Once in a while they let her, like one time when they'd let her be a junior unicorn maiden after she'd promised and double promised not to tell a soul.

"Yeah," Ari said. "She heard Carlos talking on the phone to Bucky about chopping down the grove. She was mad at him for eating up all the Dove bars so she decided to tell you. Only you weren't home so she told me."

Aurora's face was stiff and pale. She looked around at the clearing where she and Kate had pulled out all the weeds and then bordered the cleared area with smooth gray-white stones. She looked at the sacred circle in the center of the clearing with its silver unicorn and golden bowl. Then she looked at Kate. "What are we going to do?" she whispered.

Kate didn't hesitate for a minute. "We won't let them," she said. Her voice was quick and angry.

"What are we going to do to stop them?" Aurora's voice was a breathy whisper.

"Yeah, what?" Ari asked at the same moment. "What?" was a good question. It was one of the questions reporters were supposed to ask. Along with "who?" "where?" "when?" and "why?" you were supposed to ask "what?" In this case the "what" was—"*What* are you going to do to them, Kate?"

Kate's face was beginning to look bluish, as if she'd been holding her breath like a little kid having a tantrum. Ari had seen her look that way before and it generally meant someone was in real trouble. "I'll kill them," Kate said.

Ari felt the hair on the back of his neck begin to quiver. He looked at his sister. "Aurora?" he asked frantically.

Aurora was staring at Kate. "She doesn't mean *that* kind of kill," she said. "She means the kind where you—like, put a spell on them. Where you put them under a spell. That's what you mean, isn't it, Kate?"

Kate blinked several times. Then she took a deep breath. Her face began to look a little less blue. "Yeah," she said. "Like she says. We'll put a spell on them."

She looked at Aurora. Ari was looking at Aurora too. "How?" he asked. Kate nodded.

"How?" she asked. "What kind of a spell?"

"Well," Aurora said. "Let's see." She put her hands together and interlaced her fingers. Then she slowly wiggled her fingers back and forth. She always did that when she was thinking. Her flowery wreath and a swoop of crinkly hair had slipped down across her forehead, almost hiding her eyes. "Let's see," she said again. "Let me think."

Aurora and Kate were still in the Unicorn's Grove when Athena finally said good-bye to Prince and ran home to eat her breakfast. But then she came right back because the Anderson grandkids had asked her to play. They were playing on the swings in the Andersons' backyard when Mr. A. came out of the house. Mr. A., as most of the Castle Court kids called him, was a tall man with lots of white hair and a very big smile. Athena and the grandkids jumped off the swings and ran to meet him.

The grandkids said, "Hi, Grandpa," and Athena said, "Hi, Mr. A." And when he said he was on his way to check on old Prince, Athena said, "Me too."

When they got to the fence Prince was out in the middle of the pasture lying down. Mr. A. called to him and he raised his head and looked toward the fence, but he didn't get up.

"Why doesn't he come to see us?" the littlest grandkid said. "He always comes to see Athena."

"Guess the old boy is feeling tired," Mr. A. said. "You know Prince is a very old horse."

"Maybe he won't come because we don't have a

carrot," the other grandkid said. "Athena always brings him a carrot."

"I'll get him another one," Athena said, and she jumped down off the fence and ran toward home. She ran all the way to her own yard thinking about a carrot, but when she got there she saw something so interesting she forgot all about it.

Something unusual was happening in the gazebo in the backyard of number eight Castle Court. Aurora and Kate and Ari and Susie Garcia were sitting in a circle talking about something important. Athena could tell it was really important because no one was laughing or even smiling. Not even Susie, who was almost always laughing—except when she was yelling at somebody.

Athena knew that big kids don't let four-year-olds be part of something really important, so she just went quietly to her room. As soon as she got there she opened her window and leaned way out. Sometimes when she leaned out of her window she could hear what people were saying a long way off. Even as far off as the gazebo.

Athena leaned farther out of the window and strained her ears, but she still couldn't quite hear. She was holding her breath and leaning even farther when Aurora suddenly called her name. Athena almost fell out of the window.

"Athena! Come here, Athena," Aurora called again, and Athena scrambled back inside her room and came running. When she got to the gazebo Aurora said, "Sit down in the council circle, Athena." Kate looked surprised and then frowned, but Aurora just went on nodding slowly. "I have a mysterious feeling that Athena can help," she said.

Athena scooted up on the bench in the council circle, folded her hands, and tried to look serious and thoughtful. But she was so excited she could hardly sit still. She didn't know yet what mysterious thing she was going to do to help. In fact, she didn't even know yet who needed to be helped. But she felt sure that she was going to find out very soon.

Chapter

7

The Pappas gazebo was a good place to hold a mysterious council meeting because it was that kind of a place—mysterious. It had once been a pretty ordinary gazebo—a little round outdoorsy kind of room with fancy wooden decorations all around the roof. But then Athena's father painted it black and purple and decorated it with a bunch of his sculptures. So now fat lumpy things with goat heads and scorpion tails sat on the roof, a big bronze snake climbed up one of the posts, and a blobby monster with a huge mouth and lots of teeth dangled down from the ceiling.

Athena knew that some people thought that what her father had done to the gazebo was scary and terrible, but she liked it fine—except after dark. And it was just right for a mysterious council meeting—in broad daylight with lots of other people around. She squeezed her hands together and tried very hard to sit still.

After Athena joined the council no one said anything for a long time. Except for Ari, who was writing in his notebook, no one did anything either, or even moved. After a while Athena leaned over and poked him. "What are we waiting for?" she whispered.

"Shhh," he said. "We're waiting for Aurora to get a mysterious feeling about how to do the spell."

Athena didn't understand. Very, very quietly she made her lips shape the words "What's a spell?"

Ari leaned closer and whispered that they were going to do a spell that would keep first base out of the Unicorn's Grove.

Athena nodded uncertainly. She knew about unicorns of course. Unicorns were horses with one big horn. Kate and Aurora had lots of them.

"What's a grove?" she whispered.

Ari frowned and tried to scoot away. But after she asked again he whispered, "A grove is a bunch of trees where unicorns live. Like that bunch of trees at Dragoland. Only Carlos and Bucky are going to chop it down and make it into first base." Then he moved over across the circle so she couldn't ask him any more questions.

Athena thought she understood about the grove, but she still wasn't sure about the *spell.* The only *spell* she knew about was what grown-ups did when they didn't want you to know what they were talking about. Like "S-H-O-T-S." "S-H-O-T-S" was what grown-ups *spelled* when you were going to have to go to the doctor and they didn't want you to start crying before you got there. But she was pretty sure they weren't talking about that kind of a spell at the council. She bit her lip and clenched her fists and tried very hard to sit still and wait. After a while Kate started talking.

Kate was the first person at the council to start talking, and what she was talking about was shooting people with slingshots.

"I know how to make these humongous sling-shots," she said. "I mean, real killers. And we could make a fort inside the grove. We could put up sort of a wall to hide behind in the clearing and then we could pile up a bunch of rocks and when they start to cut the trees we could run out and—"

Kate crouched down on the floor of the gazebo, picked up an imaginary rock, and jumped to her feet. She pulled back an imaginary slingshot and yelled, "Okay, you nerds. You want first base? You got first base! Look out. Here it comes!" Then she shot the imaginary rock so hard she almost fell over the table.

"Yeah," Susie said. "Let's clobber them. I want to clobber Carlos."

Athena knew that Carlos was Susie's big brother. She thought it was interesting that Susie wanted to clobber him. She looked across the council circle to where Ari had moved to get away from her questions. He was sitting cross-legged on the bench and he had his writing notebook on one of his knees. He was writing something in the notebook. For a minute she practiced wanting to clobber her big brother. It wouldn't be too hard, she decided. Ari was pretty skinny, and besides he was always so busy writing it would be easy to sneak up on him—and *whack!*

Whack, she thought, looking at the way Ari's tongue was sticking out of the corner of his mouth and how he had his notebook balanced on one of his skinny knees. She shrugged. Whacking Ari didn't seem like it would be all that much fun. Maybe it would be more fun if your brother was as big as Carlos Garcia.

Aurora hadn't said anything yet. She'd been sitting very still with her eyes wide open but not seeing anything. You could tell she wasn't seeing anything by the woozy look in her eyes. The other people at the council kept looking at Aurora like they were waiting for her to say something, but she didn't. Athena wished Aurora would hurry up and tell about the spell.

Athena was still watching Ari writing in his notebook and trying hard not to squirm, when Ari suddenly said, "I have an idea. What I think we ought to do is to send a message to the PROs. We ought to send a message that we don't want them to chop down the grove. And maybe that we want to have a meeting with them to talk about it."

The other people at the council meeting looked at Ari.

Kate made a snorting noise. "Talk," she said. "It won't do any good to talk to those creeps."

Susie nodded her head hard. "You can't talk to Carlos," she said.

"How do you know?" Ari asked. "Have you ever tried it?"

Susie glared at Ari. "Of course I've tried it. He's my brother. I tried it just a few days ago and all he did was throw a ball at me."

Ari looked worried. "Carlos throws baseballs at people?"

"Basketballs," Susie said.

Ari shrugged. "Well, that's not quite as bad," he said.

"I know," Susie said, "but that's just because a basketball is what he's always carrying around. Just wait till they start playing baseball."

But Aurora didn't seem to be interested in what Susie was saying. She was looking at Ari and her eyes had stopped having the woozy look. "What would the message to the PROs say?" she asked. "What exact words?"

"Well." Ari looked at his notebook for a minute. Then he asked, "How do you spell *environment*?"

"E-n-v-i," Kate started.

"O-r-n-a-ment," Aurora went on.

Ari erased and wrote for a minute. Then he put his pencil behind his ear and arranged his notebook carefully on his knee.

"I've been doing a practice one," he said. "Maybe it could say something like this . . ." Ari opened his notebook and began to read.

Ari cleared his throat and began to read his message to the PROs in a stiff grown-up voice. "Dear PROs," he read. "This message is from a whole bunch of important people who won't let you cut down any trees at Dragoland. There are a lot of reasons why we won't let you. One reason is because of the envi-ornament and the ecology. Another reason is that the grove does not belong to you. It does not belong to us either, but we have been using it for something important for a long time and you haven't. Another reason is that there are a lot of us."

"How's that?' Ari asked.

"But there wasn't anything about a meeting," Aurora said.

"Oh yeah," Ari said. Then he stuck out the tip of his tongue again and wrote some more. He wrote for quite a while. When he was finished he read, "We would like to have a meeting to talk about it. Tonight before dinner, at the Weedpatch. Please write an answer and send it back with the messenger."

Everyone nodded, particularly Aurora. "Yes," she said. "Yes. That's really good, Ari. Take it to the Garcias' right away."

"Me?" Ari said. "I didn't say anything about being the messenger. I mean, I've gotten messages from those guys before." He clenched his fist and pretended to hit himself in the side of the head. "*Kapow!* That's a Bucky Brockhurst message. *Kapow!*" He hit himself again.

Kate looked as if she'd been holding her breath again. "I'll take the message," she said. "I'd just like to see that Bucky creep try to *kapow* me."

"No," Aurora said quickly. "That wouldn't do any good. We need to talk to them. Karate chopping them is not going to make them talk to us." Aurora looked at Susie for a minute and then shook her head. Then she looked at Athena. Athena began to feel very excited. She tried not to bounce up and down because big kids don't bounce when they are excited.

Aurora looked at her for a long time. Then she looked far away with the woozy look in her eyes again. When she looked back at Athena she said, "Athena will help us. I have a feeling Athena will help save the Unicorn's Grove."

Athena stood up as straight and tall as she could. She was very glad to find out what she could do to help. "I can do it. I can take the message to Carlos."

"Yeah. That's a great idea," Ari said. "That way nobody will get hurt. Nobody's going to clobber a four-year-old. Not even old Bucky."

Aurora's eyes were very woozy. "Athena will save the grove," she said in a whispery voice, as if she were talking to somebody in a dream.

"How?" Kate asked. "How is Athena going to do it?" But Aurora only shook her head.

Athena took the message from Ari. "I'm going to take the message," she said. "That's how."

Athena started off for the Garcias' house holding the message carefully in both hands. Just as she got to the sidewalk a car turned into Castle Court. It was the big shiny blue car that belonged to the Brockhursts. As it went past, Athena could see Bucky Brockhurst in the front seat with his father and Muffy Brockhurst in the backseat with her mother. Athena nodded knowingly. The Brockhurst family always rode that way—and everybody knew why. Everybody knew that Bucky and Muffy fought too much to ride in the same seat.

Athena, who was always very careful about cars, waited and watched until the car disappeared into the Brockhursts' garage. Then she started across the street.

Crossing the cul-de-sac, she walked very tall and straight. She didn't run or skip. Taking the message to the PROs was too important for skipping. At the planter island she stopped to unfold the paper carefully and read a few words, just to see if the message was still all right.

Even though she was only four Athena could read quite a lot of words. Aurora and Ari had been early readers and so was Athena. Athena could already read all the words in *The Cat in the Hat*. But those words were in printing. Now that Ari was in third grade he was writing most of his words in cursive. Athena knew all about cursive. She couldn't read it very well yet, but she'd heard Ari read the message out loud so that helped. She could pick out the words *trees* and *cut* and *bad*. She also found a long word that started with a *D* that probably was *Dragoland*. It made her feel very good to read such a long word in cursive. She stopped two more times to unfold the message and find the word *Dragoland*, to be sure she could still read it. Then she folded the paper very carefully and went up the walk to the Garcias' front door.

Chapter

8

While Athena was still on her way across Castle Court the back door of the Brockhurst house slammed open and Bucky shot out. He skidded to a stop, dropped down into a starting-block crouch, and kicked off into an all-out run—hundred-yard-dash practice.

At the low hedge between his house and Carlos's he practiced his hurdle-jumping technique. After he cleared the hedge he zigged and zagged clear around the Garcias' swimming pool carrying an imaginary football and skillfully avoiding half a dozen imaginary tacklers. As he zigged past a water-polo ball he grabbed it up and dribbled it across the cement part of the patio. Then, tossing the ball back toward where he'd found it, he revved up to full speed again. Just before he got to the stairs he dove headfirst into a belly slide. Jumping to his feet, he yelled, "Safe at home!" and pounded up the stairs to bang on the Garcias' back door. After a minute Carlos came out.

For a second Carlos stared in surprise. Bucky's straw-colored hair was standing on end, his face was red and sweaty, and there was a big grass stain down the front of his shirt. But that wasn't what surprised Carlos. There was nothing unusual about a sweaty, messy Bucky. What surprised Carlos was that Bucky was there at all.

"Hey, Buckaroo," he said, slapping Bucky's hand. "When did you get home? I thought you were going to be gone all day."

"Yeah, I thought so too. But Muffy fought with me so much my folks got mad and we came home early."

As Carlos led the way into the kitchen he said, "Hey, too bad. I thought you were going to get to go to a matinee."

"Yeah, I thought so too. And what's more, I'm grounded. And it's all Muffy's fault. She told Dad I kicked her."

"Oh yeah?" Carlos said. "Did you?"

"Did I what?"

"Did you kick Muffy?"

"Sure I did. But she's not supposed to tell. You're never supposed to tell adults stuff like that. Muffy knows that. But she did it anyhow so now I'm grounded." He opened the door of the Garcias' refrigerator and looked inside. "Got anything good to eat in here?" he asked. "I'm hungry."

"Not much," Carlos said. "I ate the last Dove bar this morning." He was disappointed about Bucky being grounded. "You mean you can't help with the first-base thing tomorrow?"

"No, that'll be okay. I'm not grounded tomorrow. I'm grounded right now." Bucky was pawing around in the cheese drawer. He pulled out a slice of cheddar and stuck it in his mouth.

"Right now? You're grounded right now? How come you're here then?"

"I'm not here," Bucky said. "Not officially. I just came over to tell you I couldn't come over. I'm leaving right this minute."

"Right this minute, huh?" Carlos asked.

"Yeah," Bucky said. He opened the refrigerator door again and took out another piece of cheese.

Just at that moment the front doorbell rang.

"I got to go to the door," Carlos called back over his shoulder as he left the kitchen. "My mom's washing her hair and nobody else is home. I guess you have to go home anyway."

"Yeah," Bucky said. "I have to go this minute." But he didn't. Instead he grabbed another piece of cheddar and, still munching, followed Carlos to the front door. When the big double doors swung open, Carlos thought for a second that no one was there. But then he noticed her standing beside the big potted Joshua tree. It was the little kid from across the court. He remembered the curly ponytail. The little kid from the kooky artist family. Angela, or something like that. "Hi, Angela," he said.

"Not Angela," she said. "Athena."

"Whatever," Carlos said. "Did you want to see Susie? She's not at home."

"I know that," Athena said. "She's at the council. I came to see you."

Behind Carlos, Bucky laughed—"Hee, hee, hee" —the way he always did to tease people. "Hee, hee, hee. She came to see you, dude. You got a new girlfriend, Garcia?"

The little kid frowned at Bucky. "You're a creep," she said.

Bucky looked surprised—and then angry—and then confused.

Carlos couldn't help grinning—because nobody dared to call Bucky Brockhurst a creep. Anybody who called Bucky Brockhurst anything he didn't like got slugged—immediately. No questions asked. Anybody, that is, except this little bitty kid.

The little kid handed Carlos a piece of paper. "Here," she said. "I brought you a message."

The message was written in pencil on a page from a notebook. It was a little kid's handwriting, fat and scribbly. Like someone who hadn't been writing cursive very long. Carlos read the message. He laughed and handed it to Bucky. Bucky laughed too.

"We'll be there," Carlos said. "Dragoland. Tonight. Before dinner. You tell this *big* bunch of people we'll be there." Then he remembered about Bucky being grounded. "Or I'll be there, anyway. This—" He stopped. He seriously considered saying, "This creep," but then he decided against it. "This—dude is grounded."

Bucky shrugged and grinned. "Grounded, schmounded. Count me in. I'll be there."

"You're supposed to write it," the little kid said. "On the back of the paper."

"You write it," Bucky said. "I got to get home."

So Carlos found a pencil and wrote, "We will be there," on the back of the notebook paper and signed it "Carlos Garcia." The little kid folded it up carefully and went off across the circle to her house.

"Crazy kid," Carlos said. He was talking to Bucky but when he turned around Bucky was disappearing down the hall at a run. A second later Carlos heard the refrigerator door open—and then close. He grinned. Some more of his mom's cheddar cheese was disappearing too.

Chapter

9

The council meeting ended right after Athena came back from the Garcias' with Carlos's signature on the message. Athena was disappointed. She really liked being part of a council. But Susie and Kate both had to go home.

"My mom said I could only stay for an hour," Susie said. "I'm supposed to be finishing my book report."

Kate Nicely jumped up and looked at her watch. "Wow, me too. I have to help Carson clean up his room. Aurora. Aurora! Hey, snap out of it! I'm leaving!"

Aurora, who was still sitting cross-legged on the bench with her hands on her knees, blinked rapidly and came back to earth. She slid down off the bench and followed Kate across the lawn and down the Pappases' driveway. Kate kept glancing at Aurora. She looked strange, her eyes wide and empty—and sad. Very, very sad.

"Look," Kate said. "It *was* about to happen. The unicorn, I mean. I'll bet it was almost there when Ari busted in like that and scared it away."

Aurora sighed and nodded. "Almost," she said in a tragic voice. "And now it's too late. Now the grove will be gone and the unicorn will never—"

"No, the grove won't be gone," Kate said as quickly and firmly as she could. "Like you said, something's going to happen to stop those stupid PROs from cutting it down. You said there would be like some sort of magic spell that we could put on them to stop them from cutting it down."

"Yes." Aurora sounded uncertain. "Yes, the spell. I have to think about it some more." She turned back toward her house. "I have to go think about it," she said over her shoulder. Kate watched until Aurora had disappeared into the Pappases' house before she crossed Castle Avenue and headed for home.

As she crossed the street and went up the path to her own front door Kate's mind was going in circles. *It isn't fair*, she kept thinking. It wasn't fair that those jerks could just all of a sudden decide to chop down the grove when it had been Kate's and Aurora's for months and months. Years, actually. At least it had been Aurora's for years and years. Kate knew that was true because Aurora had told her so.

"I was about three years old when I discovered it," Aurora had said, "and I knew what it was right away. I absolutely knew."

"You knew about the unicorn?" Kate had asked.

Aurora had shaken her head slowly and thoughtfully. "No, not the unicorn. Not right at first. I just knew it was a very special, magical place. The grove has been my very special place since I was three years old."

Remembering what Aurora had said, and remembering over and over again how shocked and sad her face had been when she heard what the PROs were planning, Kate clenched her fists. "No they won't!" she whispered. "The spell will work—but just in case it doesn't I'm going to make some plans of my own. I'll think of something even better than slingshots. Just as soon as I finish vacuuming Carson's room."

Kate's brother, Carson Nicely, was a short, near-sighted seven-year-old weirdo. Actually their father had forbidden Kate to use the *weirdo* word about Carson. Being a lawyer made her father extra particular about the way words like *weirdo* were used, and what he always said was there were a lot better ways for Kate to describe her little brother. The words he suggested were *extraordinary person* or *original character* or even *free spirit*. Kate still thought *weirdo* was a lot closer to the truth.

Like the bug thing, for instance. Carson collected them, and not just your ordinary, everyday beetles and butterflies either. Carson's collection included every kind of ant, bee, worm, spider, and slimy slug known to mankind. He collected them in his room in beehives, ant farms, cages, terrariums, matchboxes, and mustard jars. Anything you touched, or bumped into, or sat on in Carson's room probably had a bug or two in it. And that's if you were lucky. If you weren't lucky it could be a whole swarm.

And then there were the snakes to consider. As if bugs weren't bad enough, Carson also collected lizards and snakes. In fact, some things in his collection were there just because they were waiting to be fed to the lizards and snakes. Just thinking about Carson's collection made your skin crawl, and smelling it could ruin your whole day.

While Kate was still standing outside Carson's room trying to prepare herself for the smell, Tiffany came out of her room and went down the hall. Tiffany, Kate's older sister, was a teenager. A clever, sneaky teenager who had gotten out of having to help Carson clean his room by claiming she had a disease. Something called Bug-o-phobia. Tiffany claimed that if she so much as looked at Carson's collection she would probably go into a coma and die. So now Tiffany was headed for the backyard in her new swimsuit, and Kate was stuck with vacuuming Carson's room. Kate wished she'd thought of Bug-o-phobia first.

"Sneak," Kate whispered under breath at Tiffany's disappearing back. Then she squared her shoulders and opened the door to Carson's room.

"Okay, Bro'," Kate said. "Here I am."

Carson was sitting on the floor in the middle of what looked like the city dump—and smelled like a rotting compost pile. His glasses had slid down to the end of his nose and there was a desperate look on his round, pudgy face. "I tried," he said. "I just didn't know where to start."

Kate looked around at the ant farms, fly traps, terrariums, hives, jars, and bottles. "Let's see," she said. "You can start by moving everything to that side of the room while I go get the vacuum." She headed for the door and then stopped. "Everything except the beehive, that is."

Carson's beehive was fitted into a window, and the only opening was out-of-doors so they couldn't get inside the house and sting people. At least that was the theory. Three of the hive's walls were made of wood but the inside one was of glass so you

61

could watch everything the bees did inside the hive. Which was interesting, in a way—if you liked spying on the private lives of bees. Actually it was a pretty disgusting sight.

Carson nodded eagerly. "Okay," he said. "Move everything. Over there. All except the beehive. Okay." He grabbed up a big cage and staggered across the room.

The trouble with Carson, Kate thought as she went down the hall to get the vacuum, *is that he just isn't organized.* He'd probably been trying to clean up his room all morning without getting anywhere. But Kate herself was very organized. And what she was going to organize next was a foolproof way to defend the Unicorn's Grove.

A few minutes later as Kate was carefully vacuuming around some shelves full of things she didn't even want to look at, she stopped suddenly and turned off the switch. "Hey, Carson," she said, "I just had an idea."

Carson carefully put down the ant farm he was carrying before he asked, "What idea?"

"Well," Kate said, "I guess you know that Edna told Mom she won't clean your room anymore? You know, because of Slinky?"

Edna was the Nicelys' cleaning lady, and Slinky was Carson's biggest boa constrictor.

Carson nodded sadly. "Mom told me," he said. "I guess Edna isn't used to snakes."

"And you know what Mom said about keeping your room clean or else you'd have to get rid of"— Kate gestured around the room—"a lot of this stuff."

Carson sighed and nodded even more sadly.

"Well," Kate went on. "How would you like to have me help you clean your room every week?"

Carson's pudgy face lit up in a big smile. "Okay," he said.

Kate nodded. "Well, then I will. But there's just one little thing I'd like you to do for me."

Behind their little round glasses, Carson's eyes narrowed suspiciously. "What do I have to do?" he said.

Chapter

10

All that afternoon Carlos phoned Eddy every half hour to see if he'd gotten home, and every time he got only the phone machine. Once he even went over and knocked on the door of the Wongs' house just to be sure. But of course Eddy wasn't there. Carlos couldn't see why it was taking so long just to visit relatives. It was getting later and later and before long it would be time to go to the Weedpatch and find out what this dumb meeting thing was all about.

The meeting would start, and Eddy still wouldn't be home, and Bucky was more or less grounded—so maybe Carlos would be all alone. Toward five o'clock Carlos started hanging out in the backyard hoping that Bucky would get himself ungrounded or else sneak out while his dad wasn't looking. Bucky was usually pretty good at that kind of thing. But as time went by with no sign of Eddy or Bucky, Carlos began to feel more and more worried. He paced up and down beside the pool worrying and thinking.

For a while he even thought of just not going himself. Of course he had said that he would be there. He'd written it down right there on the back of the paper. So not showing up would be breaking his word. But breaking his word to—whom? Who was the "whole bunch" of people who supposedly didn't want those trees cut down? Some of them must be the other Pappas kids—Aurora and Ari. The Pappases were always doing crazy things. But that was hardly a whole bunch of people. Who else might be in on it?

And then there was another question. A more mysterious one. Whoever they were, how did they know about his idea to cut down a few trees at Dragoland? He hadn't mentioned it to anyone except Bucky. And right after that Bucky had gone to town with his folks, so he couldn't have told anyone. The whole thing was pretty mysterious.

Just as Carlos was about to give up and go inside, everything started happening at once. It started with a muffled thudding noise and a loud whisper that came from the Brockhurst side of the hedge. "Shhh," the voice said. "Meet me out front."

"Okay," Carlos whispered back and started around to the front of the house. And then just as

Bucky crawled out of a rhododendron bush in the Brockhursts' front yard, a car drove into the circle. It was the Wongs' Toyota. So suddenly the three PROs were together again—and just in the nick of time.

Carlos and Bucky dashed across the circle just as the Wongs' car was pulling into their garage. Eddy was only halfway out of the backseat when they grabbed him and started dragging him down the driveway.

"Hey, what's up?" he asked. "What's going on?"

Carlos and Bucky were both talking at once. Bucky was babbling something about hatchets and Carlos kept saying something about a meeting. A meeting that was about to happen very soon and he, Eddy, was supposed to be there.

"Eddy! Carlos! Bucky!" It was Eddy's dad calling. "Where are you boys going?"

Carlos turned loose of Eddy's arm and went back to talk to Eddy's dad. "We just need to talk to Eddy for a few minutes, Mr. Wong," he said. "We won't be long."

Eddy's dad looked at his watch. "All right, for just ten minutes," he said. "But no more than that. No basketball tonight. You hear me, Eddy? No basketball."

"No basketball, Mr. Wong," Carlos called back.

"We promise. We're in a hurry too." Bucky went on pulling Eddy by one arm while Carlos pushed from behind.

"Hey, what's going on? Where are we going?" Eddy kept saying. "Stop shoving. If you guys don't tell me where we're going, I'm going to go home."

But he wasn't going to go home until Carlos and Bucky wanted him to because they were bigger than he was. Eddy Wong was as good an athlete as Bucky and Carlos. He just wasn't as big.

"Come on, Eddy," Carlos said. "We have to go to a meeting. A meeting about this great idea I was trying to tell you about this morning. Remember? About where we could have a baseball diamond?"

Suddenly Eddy quit struggling. Eddy really liked baseball. He was a good batter and he had a great arm, and being kind of short didn't matter as much in baseball. Just once in a while Eddy would really like to play something where he could be the best.

"Yeah? Yeah?" he said. "What about a baseball diamond? And who are we meeting with?"

"Who?" Bucky said. "Yeah. That's a good question."

But by then they had climbed into and out of the Pit and were starting across the Weedpatch.

"I told you," Eddy said to Carlos. "This place just

isn't big enough. Remember? Web measured it with his surveyor's stuff."

Eddy's little brother, Webster Wong, who was only eight years old, knew how to do surveying because he happened to be a genius. "Remember," Eddy went on, "Web measured it both ways and it's just not big enough. That bunch of trees over there is right where first base ought to be. That bunch right over there where—" He stopped and stared. "Hey, look," he said.

"Look at what? Bucky said. "I didn't see anything."

"Me neither," Carlos said.

Eddy looked from Bucky to Carlos and back again. "Are you sure? I saw something kind of peeking out of that bunch of bamboo. Something like a face."

"Oh yeah? Like whose face?" Bucky said.

"I don't know. I didn't see it well enough."

"Well, it probably was one of the people we're supposed to be meeting with. You know, about the baseball diamond thing." Eddy still looked blank so Carlos started filling him in. "See, the thing is, I had this great idea about how we could chop down that whole grove over there. It wouldn't be hard. It's just bamboo and those little skinny trees. And then we could put first base right there and then the Weed-patch would be big enough. Wouldn't it?"

Eddy's eyes lit up. "Yeah," he said. "I think it would be. But those trees don't belong to us. We might get in trouble."

"Trouble, schmouble," Bucky said. "Those trees don't belong to anyone, except maybe the Drago-mans. And they're never here. They don't even know the trees are there."

Eddy nodded. "But what about this meeting then? What's that all about?"

So Carlos told Eddy all about the note—and more or less what it said about a big bunch of people who didn't want the trees cut down. He finished the story by saying, "But the really weird part is we don't have any idea how these nerds, whoever they are, found out what we were planning to do. We didn't tell anybody. Did we, Bucky?"

Just at that moment Eddy saw it again. "Look," he yelled. "There it is again. Two of them this time. I saw two faces." But Carlos and Bucky hadn't looked soon enough.

"That does it," Carlos said. "I'm going in there and find out who it is. You guys stay here to catch them when they run out."

"Okay," Bucky said. "I'll stay right here and you

69

go over that way, Eddy." As Carlos headed for the grove Bucky crouched down like a football player getting ready for the snap. "I'm going to tackle the first thing that runs out of there," he yelled.

Carlos disappeared into the grove.

There was no path. Slender tree trunks crowded around him, and thick blobby clusters of leaves were everywhere. Leaves trailed across Carlos's face, blocking his vision. He was trying to push them away from his face when suddenly he found himself in a small clearing no bigger than a room in a house. All around him dense stands of bamboo and young acacia trees made a solid green wall. Around the clearing, at the foot of the green wall, there was a kind of border of smooth white stones. The grass in the clearing was short and green, almost like a lawn. And right in the middle of the lawn there was something long and silvery. Long and silvery and—*alive*.

As Carlos stared in horror the long silvery thing raised its big oval head and pointed it right in his direction. It was a—*snake!* An absolutely humongous snake. Carlos yelled and smashed his way back through the green wall.

Bucky and Eddy were waiting for him just outside the grove. When he burst out through the bamboo Bucky said, "Hey, man. Where were you? What happened?"

"A snake," Carlos started to yell, but for a moment nothing came out. Bucky and Eddy were staring at him strangely. He waved his arms, opened his mouth several times, made a squeaking noise, and then tried again. "A snake," he finally managed. "There's this huge snake in there. About ten feet long."

"Wow!" Bucky said. "A rattlesnake?"

"I d-d-don't know," Carlos stammered. "It was just big! Real big."

Bucky started looking around. he picked up a stick, balanced it in his hand, and then threw it back down again. Then he turned suddenly and ran back toward the Pit. A minute later he came back carrying a shovel and a couple of big sticks. Handing the sticks to Carlos and Eddy, he yelled, "Come on, you dudes. Let's go chop up that . . ."

Bucky's voice trailed off in midsentence. ". . . snake," he whispered. Then he gulped and said, "Oh, hi, Dad. I just had to come over here to tell Carlos something. I was coming right home. Here I come."

Mr. Brockhurst was standing near the brick foundation at the back of the Pit. He didn't look happy. And just at that moment a bell started ringing. The bell was the one that hung on the Wongs' back porch, and when it rang it meant that Eddy and Web had better get home. Fast.

So that took care of both Eddy and Bucky. Carlos was left all alone just outside of the grove. For a moment he stood staring at the dense wall of quivering green leaves. He was remembering something. He was remembering that Carson Nicely had snakes. Big ones. And that Carson was Kate's brother—and that Kate Nicely and Aurora Pappas were best friends. And of course the little Athena twerp was Aurora's sister. It was all beginning to come together.

"Okay, you guys," he shouted. "We'll be back tomorrow with hatchets and chain saws and—and—with a snake-killing dog too."

Actually he didn't know if Lump would kill a snake. As far as he knew, Lump had never met one. But Carlos felt sure Lump *could* if he wanted to. He was certainly big enough. And of course there wasn't really any chain saw. But it sounded good. "We'll be back tomorrow for sure," he yelled again.

He started to walk away but after a minute he turned around and walked backward. Nothing moved in the grove. "You asked for it," he yelled. "This means war."

Chapter

11

From her hiding place in the clump of bamboo Kate Nicely watched Carlos Garcia as he finally stopped waving his arms and shouting about chain saws and snake-killing dogs and disappeared into the bushes that surrounded the Pit.

"Sure you will, stupid," she whispered. Then she raised her voice and said, "He's just bluffing, Carson. He's just trying to scare us. Carson! Carson?" There was no answer and nothing moved in the Unicorn's Grove clearing. Both Carson and Slinky had disappeared.

It wasn't until Kate had searched the grove thoroughly and pushed her way back out into the open that she saw him—a small dumpy figure marching off toward home with about ten feet of boa constrictor wrapped around his neck. She could tell he was angry. Carson Nicely didn't get mad easily but when he did—look out!

"Carson," she called. "Carson. Come back here."

She ran after him but even when she caught up he just kept on stomping and glaring straight ahead.

"Look, Carson," she said. "I wouldn't have let them hurt Slinky."

"They were going to chop him," Carson said. "With a shovel. You didn't tell me Slinky might get chopped."

They were almost to the sidewalk, with Carson still stomping and glaring, when they suddenly ran into all the rest of the council—Aurora, Ari and Athena Pappas, and Susie Garcia—on their way to the meeting. On their way to a meeting that hadn't happened and now probably never would. The four of them stopped to stare at Carson as he stomped past with Slinky wrapped around his shoulders.

"Oooh. Look at Slinky," Athena said.

"Yikes!" Susie squealed. "Stay away from me. Stay away from me with that thing, Carson Nicely."

"What happened?" Ari said. He twisted his fanny pack around and started to pull out a notebook.

Kate sighed. She waited until Carson and Slinky had disappeared across Castle Court and the other kids had stopped staring after him before she sighed again and began to explain. ". . . I just had this—well, I guess it was a dumb idea about how to get rid of the PROs." She looked at Aurora. "I just remembered all of a sudden about the way Carlos kind of freaked out that day when Matt brought that little old garter snake to school. Remember?" Kate made a scared face and jumped back like Carlos had done when he saw the snake. "Remember that, Aurora?"

Aurora nodded.

"Well," Kate went on, "I suddenly thought that if he saw Slinky in the grove he might just, well, you know, kind of lose interest in the whole project. So I got Carson to bring him over here. But it didn't work the way I wanted it to. Old Brockhurst got this shovel and started yelling about chopping Slinky up. And I guess he might have done it too, except his father showed up really angry. I mean, he looked *mad*. But Carson heard what Brockhurst was yelling about chopping Slinky and it really freaked him out. He's crazy about that dumb snake."

Ari was writing something in his notebook. "How do you spell *freaked*?" he asked Kate.

"F-r-e . . . ," Kate started—and then stopped and glared. "Look, Ari," she said. "This isn't a newspaper story. This is real life. And we have a real-life problem. Like, those creeps are going to come back here tomorrow with saws and axes and—"

"I thought we were going to have a meeting," Aurora said in her soft, breathy voice. "I thought we were going to try to talk to them about ecology and the environment and about how the . . ." She stopped and shrugged. "Well, I guess not."

"Yeah," Kate said. "I *double* guess not. Not if you were thinking of trying to tell them about the . . ." She looked around and lowered her voice and mouthed, "the unicorn."

But Athena had very good ears. "The what?" she said. "The unicorn? You said unicorn. I heard you. What about the unicorn?"

"Shhh," Aurora said to Athena. "I'll tell you about it later." Then she said to Kate, "So there's not going to be a meeting then?"

Kate nodded ruefully. She felt bad about ruining the meeting, even if it wouldn't have worked. "It probably wouldn't have done any good anyway," she said.

"Yeah," Susie said. "I told you so. I said it was no use talking to those guys."

Ari stopped writing in his notebook. "So," he said, "what's going to happen next?"

Kate looked at Aurora. She wanted to ask about the spell but didn't know if she should. But Aurora guessed. "No," she said. "I can't get it back. I had this mysterious feeling about something that was going to happen. Something about . . ." She stopped and looked at Athena.

"About me," Athena said proudly.

Aurora nodded. "But the feeling's gone now. I've been trying and trying, but I can't get it back." She shook her head slowly, her gray eyes dark with despair. "I just can't."

"Look," Kate said. "Don't worry about it. We can handle those crummy nerds. We'll make them wish they never heard of our grove or the Weedpatch. Or baseball. We'll make them wish they never even heard of baseball."

Susie jumped around shadowboxing the empty air. "Yeah," she said. "And Dove bars. I'm going to make them wish they never heard of Dove bars too."

Aurora stared at Susie and then at Kate. She looked at Athena, who was bouncing up and down excitedly, and at Ari, who was writing in his notebook. "If I could only . . . ," she said. They all stopped what they were doing and looked at her hopefully, but after a moment she only shook her head.

Chapter

12

By the time Carlos got home he was feeling hungry so he went right to the refrigerator. His mind always seemed to work better when he was eating—and at the moment he had lots to think about. But the big Dove bar box was empty and so was the cheese bin. He vaguely remembered eating the last of the Dove bars, and of course he knew what had happened to the cheese. Or, in this case, "who" had happened to the cheese.

Right at that moment a voice said, "What happened to all the cheese?" Strangely enough, the voice wasn't Carlos's. Actually it belonged to his mom, Brigitta Garcia, who, he suddenly noticed, was there in the kitchen stirring something on the stove. "I was going to use it for the enchiladas," she went on. "Do you know anything about it?"

Carlos winced. He hated catch-22's like this. Catch-22's where you either had to rat on someone or else tell a lie. "Well," he said. "I think Bucky might have eaten some of it when he was over here. He said he was hungry."

Then his mom, who was usually pretty cheerful for a person with four kids, turned around looking very uncheerful. "Why did you let him, Carlos?" she said. "Why didn't you tell him to go home and raid his own refrigerator?"

Another catch-22. This time where you either had to tell a lie or tell your mom you were afraid to ask someone who was supposed to be one of your best friends to go home. Let alone tell him to get his dirty paws out of your refrigerator. Carlos opened his mouth, shut it again—and was saved by the bell. Saved by having the door to the garage open and his father and brothers come in—while, at the same moment, his little sister suddenly appeared from the front of the house. In the confusion Carlos snuck out of the kitchen and headed for the upstairs phone.

Carlos called Eddy first. When Eddy answered the phone the first thing Carlos said was, "What about tomorrow?"

"What do you mean, what about tomorrow?" Eddy said.

"You know. Like we told you. Tomorrow we're going to chop down those trees. You're going to be there, aren't you?"

"Yeah, sure," Eddy said. "But what about the snake? You said there was a snake in there."

"There was. A humongous one, like a python or something. But I think I got that figured out too. I'll bet it was a tame one. You know that little Nicely kid? Carlson, or something like that. He has pet snakes, doesn't he? And Kate Nicely is real tight with the Pappases. So those Pappas dweebs are probably behind this whole thing."

"Yeah, Carson has snakes," Eddy said. "His name is Carson. But why do you suppose they don't want us to cut down that little bunch of trees? I mean, what's in it for them?"

Carlos had thought about that a little. "I don't know for sure, but the note said something about ecology and that sort of thing. They're probably just a bunch of ecology nuts."

"Hmm," Eddy said. "Well, what do you want me to do?"

"Well, you don't have a chain saw, do you? Or an ax?"

Eddy laughed. "Me? 'Fraid not."

"That's okay. Bucky has this hatchet. We can just

take turns with the hatchet. But what we need is some more people."

"Why?" Eddy asked. "Why do we need more people if we only have one hatchet?"

"Because they do. At least they said they did in the note. And we know for sure they have all three of the Pappases and Kate and Carlson Nicely."

"Carson," Eddy said.

"Okay, Carson. Anyway, the thing is, we may need to have enough guys to keep their guys from bothering the one who is doing the chopping."

"How about your brothers?" Eddy asked.

"Well," Carlos thought about it for a minute. It would be great to have two big guys like Rafe and Gabe on their side. But the more Carlos thought about it the more he knew it wouldn't happen. Rafe was too old and too busy being a big hotshot high-school football star. And Gabe? Carlos had a sneaking feeling that Gabe, who once had made up a song about saving the rain forests, might wind up being on the other side. For a moment he had a quick flash of Gabe playing his guitar and singing about saving the rain forest of Castle Court.

"Naw," he said. "I guess not. How about Web?"

Eddy laughed. "Web?" He laughed again, as if it was a big joke.

Actually Carlos saw what he meant. Webster Wong, who could handle things like test tubes and microscopes and computers like a pro, wouldn't be all that good at facing up to a bunch of angry nuts— ecology or otherwise. And besides, Web and Carson were kind of alike in some ways. "Aren't Web and Carson friends?" he asked.

"Not exactly," Eddy said. "Carson comes over here sometimes and Web goes to his house, but I think they're mostly just visiting each other's collections."

"Well, that's okay then. Ask Web if he'll come and be on our side."

Eddy didn't say anything for a minute, and when he did he didn't sound too enthusiastic. "Yeah, well this whole thing is beginning to sound pretty complicated. I mean, their side has secret weapons, like Karate Kate. And snakes too. I'm not too crazy about big snakes, even tame ones."

Carlos knew what Eddy meant. Everyone at Beaumont knew about Kate Nicely and all her karate belts, and he also certainly knew what Eddy meant about not liking snakes. But he couldn't let Eddy back out. "Look," he said. "I'll bring Lump. Lump will take care of that snake."

"Yeah?" Eddy was obviously doubtful. "Lump kills snakes?"

It was Carlos's turn to laugh a phony laugh. "Lump?" he said. "You don't believe Lump could kill that snake? That's funny. Lump could probably kill that snake just by sitting on it."

They both laughed. "So," Carlos went on, "our side has a snake-killing dog. And don't forget, if Karate Kate is their secret weapon, we have one too. I mean Bucky Brockhurst, the toughest dude at Beaumont School. Our side has Bucky Brockhurst."

"Yeah," Eddy said doubtfully. "If he's not grounded. His dad sounded pretty mad."

"Oh, he won't be grounded," Carlos said. "Or at least if he is he'll find a way to get out of it. Bucky's good at that sort of thing. I'll bet he's already thought of a way to get out of it. I'll call him and find out."

"Okay," Eddy said. "You call him." But he didn't sound too enthusiastic.

When Carlos called the Brockhurst's number and Bucky's sister answered the phone, he almost hung up without saying anything. The thing was, he knew Muffy wouldn't call Bucky to the phone if she were mad at him, which she usually was, more or less. And it was probably *more* at the moment— since he'd just been grounded for kicking her. But by thinking very quickly, Carlos came up with a possible solution to that problem too.

"Oh, hi, Muffy," he said. "It's Carlos."

"Yeah, I can tell." Muffy's voice was cold and suspicious.

"Don't hang up," Carlos said quickly. "I've got an offer for you. How about—a quarter?"

"A quarter—for what?" Muffy's voice was not quite as cold.

"You know," Carlos said. "For telling Bucky I want to talk to him."

"He's grounded. He's not supposed to talk to anybody, on the phone or anything."

"Oh." Carlos was really disappointed. "Well, I guess I'll just have to wait until—"

"Fifty cents." Muffy said. "For fifty cents I'll get him to the phone."

A few minutes later Bucky's voice said, "Hi, dude. What's up?"

"Oh, hi," Carlos said. "I just thought we ought to talk about tomorrow. I thought that—"

"Hello? Hello?" Bucky said. "Are you still there?"

"Yeah, I'm still here," Carlos said.

"Okay. I just heard a clicking noise, like maybe you were hanging up."

"Yeah," Carlos said. "I heard it too. But it wasn't

me. Something's been wrong with the phone lately. It keeps making funny noises. Anyway, I wanted to talk to you about tomorrow. It looks like we might be in for some trouble. You know, from those dudes who sent us that note.'' He went on then to tell Bucky his theory about the snake being a pet one and about why he thought the three Pappases and the two Nicelys—and the snake—might be there tomorrow to try to keep the PROs from cutting down any trees. ''I think they're planning to try to scare us away,'' he said.

''Oh yeah?'' Bucky's voice was suddenly so loud Carlos had to hold the phone away from his ear. ''They think they can scare us away, do they? Hee, hee, hee! That's pretty funny. If they think that snake is going to scare *me*, they're really wacko. A baseball bat will take care of that dude. Or maybe I'll just shoot that snake full of holes. I'll just bring my—''

''Look, Brockhurst,'' Carlos was saying. ''Look. You won't have to bring baseball bats or pellet guns. I thought if we just had some more people—and if I brought Lump . . . I thought Lump . . . Lump could . . .''

But Bucky wasn't listening. Instead he just went on raving about baseball bats and pellet guns, and when Carlos tried to tell him he didn't think any of that stuff was a good idea, he just wouldn't listen. When Carlos finally gave up and said good-bye he still wasn't sure Bucky had heard a word he had said.

After dinner that night Carlos went out on the deck. It was a nice warm night and a reflection of the moon was shining up out of the swimming pool. On warm nights the deck was a nice place to sit and think. Or worry about the fact that he had been the one to start this whole baseball diamond mess in the first place. He didn't see how he could back out now, even if he really wanted to. And part of him wanted to—mostly because of Bucky. Like he'd told Eddy, Bucky Brockhurst was a secret weapon, all right. The kind that just might backfire.

Chapter

13

Ari Pappas was in the kitchen fixing himself a banana and peanut butter sandwich when the phone rang. He answered it, quietly of course. Ari always answered the phone quietly even if he knew it wasn't for him. He'd gotten some of his best story material that way. As he picked up the phone he heard his mother say, "Oh, hello, Susie. Hold on a minute. I'll call her."

Ari went on listening. He heard his mom calling and then Aurora picking up the phone and saying hello. What he heard next was very interesting. The first thing Susie said was, "Aurora. There's going to be a gun. I just heard Carlos and Bucky Brockhurst talking on the phone, and Bucky is going to bring a gun tomorrow. To Dragoland. When they come to chop down the grove."

"A gun?" Aurora's voice was a stunned whisper.

"Well, it's a pellet gun. But he said it could shoot holes in Slinky. And they're going to have baseball bats and hatchets too." Her voice rose to a wail. "What are we going to do? Do we have a gun? Does our side have a gun?"

"No," said Aurora. "We can't have a gun. A gun wouldn't help at all."

"Why not?" Susie wailed. "If they have one I don't see why we can't. Why can't we? My dad has one somewhere. I'm going to look for it."

"No, no," Aurora said. "Listen, Susie. You mustn't. You mustn't even touch it. If you even touch it you—"

"What?" Susie asked. "If I even touch it—what?"

"If you do—you can't ever be a unicorn maiden," Aurora said. "Unicorns hate and despise guns. If you even touch one the smell will be on your hands for the rest of your life. You can't ever get it off, and the unicorn will never let you come near it."

There was a long silent pause. "Really?" Susie said at last. "Really, Aurora? How do you know?"

"I just do," Aurora said. "I know about things like that."

"But what *can* we do?" Susie was wailing. "What are we going to do?"

"We won't do anything," Aurora said. "We'll just go to the grove and when they come we'll just walk out in front of it and hold hands, and we'll tell them—"

"But they'll shoot us." Susie's voice was almost a shriek.

"No, they won't. You said Bucky was going to bring the gun to shoot Slinky. And we just won't bring Slinky. He might shoot a snake, but he won't shoot us."

"Yes, he will," Susie moaned. "That Bucky Brockhurst will shoot anything. I know. I saw him shoot a robin once."

For a moment no one spoke. Ari could hear sharp, shaky breathing. Then Susie said, "I'm going to call Kate. I'm going to call Kate and tell her about the gun and everything."

"No," Aurora said quickly. "No, don't call Kate. I'll tell her tomorrow. Let me—"

But Susie had already hung up the phone.

Ari went on listening until he heard Aurora hang up. Then he hung up too, waited a minute, and picked up the phone again. Sure enough he heard Aurora dialing and then a busy signal. The busy signal went on and on and on. After a long time Ari gave up and went back to his banana and peanut butter sandwich.

While he was eating the sandwich and later when he was reading the funny papers Ari remembered to pick up the phone now and then to see if Aurora might be talking to Kate. But he must have just missed them, because about an hour later when he went to Aurora's room he found out they'd already talked. Aurora was sitting on her window seat staring out the window. "Have you talked to Kate yet?" Ari asked. "I was listening when you were talking to Susie."

Aurora nodded. "I know," she said. "I knew you were listening." She sighed. "And I did talk to Kate —after she finally finished talking to Susie."

"I thought you might have," Ari said, "but I didn't hear you. What did she say? What's she going to do?"

Aurora shook her head slowly back and forth. Then she turned and stared out the window for quite a long time. When she turned back, her face was puckered with worry. "Ari," she said. "I'm afraid. I'm afraid there's going to be a fight."

Ari nodded. "Yeah," he said. "A big one with a bunch of people on each side. Like a war almost." He thought for a moment before he told Aurora good night and headed for his own room. He'd just thought of a good title for the big story he was working on. The one about the Unicorn's Grove and the baseball diamond.

Chapter
14

The next morning Ari got up early and made a bulletproof vest. Then he went looking for Aurora. She wasn't in her room or in the bathroom, but when he got to the kitchen there she was, standing by the phone.

"Oh, hi," Ari said, feeling very relieved. "I almost thought you'd gone without me." He stared at Aurora. "You look awful," he said.

Aurora was wearing one of their father's oil-stained work shirts over polka-dot tights, and there was a wide sequin-covered stretch belt around her skinny waist. There were dark circles around her eyes and her huge mop of sun-streaked hair looked bunched and tousled. "I couldn't sleep," she said.

"Yeah, me too," Ari said. "So I got up and made me a bulletproof vest. Do you want me to make you one? I have another phone book." Ari's vest was a phone book tied around his neck by some shoestrings so that it hung down and covered most of his chest.

Aurora looked at the phone book doubtfully. "That's a bulletproof vest?" she asked.

"Sure," Ari said. "You know how people are always getting saved because the bullet hits the Bible in their pocket? So—a phone book is even thicker than a Bible and a whole lot bigger."

Aurora smiled faintly. "It does look pretty—big," she said. She looked around the room nervously. "I left a note for Mom," she said. "They're still asleep. But I think we'd better go. I called Kate but her mother said she and Carson had gone out already. For a walk, she said."

"To the grove?" Ari asked.

"Probably," Aurora said and started toward the back door. Ari followed her.

"Where's Athena?" Ari asked. "She wanted to come too."

"She's gone to visit Prince. I told her we wouldn't be going to the grove for quite a while, so she could take her time. I don't think she ought to be there anyway. Not if there are really going to be guns and things like that."

"Yeah, I guess not," Ari said, but what he was thinking was that Athena probably *should* be there. After all, she got away with taking the note to the

PROs without any trouble, which was pretty amazing. Maybe she could do something like that again. "But I thought you said Athena was going to be the one to save the grove?" he said.

"I know." Aurora shook her head. "I thought so. It was so clear for a second. But I can't get it back. I don't know. Maybe I was wrong. Anyway, she said she'd meet us there later," Aurora said. "At the grove. After she's finished taking Prince his carrot."

They had reached Dragoland by then and as they went down the path, through the Pit and out into the Weedpatch, they saw nobody at all. It wasn't until they had started pushing their way into the bamboo thicket that they saw Kate and Carson—and Susie too. Actually they heard them first.

"Halt. Who goes there?" they heard Kate's voice saying just before they got to the clearing.

"Kate?" Aurora said. "It's us. Ari and me."

"Oh, okay. Stay right where you are. We'll come and get you." A minute later Kate appeared. She was wearing a karate tunic over her shorts and two of her karate belts around her middle. Susie and Carson were right behind her. There was no sign of Slinky.

"Where's Slinky?" Ari asked.

Carson just shook his head and let Kate answer for him. "He's not here. Carson wouldn't bring any of his snakes. But he came himself, anyway, because I'm doing something for him. Carson helped with the booby trap. Didn't you, Carson?"

Carson nodded. Then he leaned forward and pointed at Ari's chest. "Phone book?" he asked in a puzzled tone of voice. But Ari was too busy thinking about booby traps to explain.

"Booby trap? You guys made a booby trap?" he asked in his best reporter's tone of voice, polite and not too nosey. His hand was already reaching back for his notebook when he realized it wasn't there. In the excitement he'd forgotten to wear his fanny pack. He'd just have to remember all the important details. "Is something going to explode?" he asked politely.

"No." Kate shook her head regretfully. "Nothing actually explodes. It's just a string that pulls a bunch of tin cans down on your head if you trip over it. See—there it is."

Ari saw it then, a thin black string stretched across the path into the clearing—and up above, a bundle of tin cans dangling from a limb.

"Mostly it's just to warn us that they're coming," Kate was saying. "So we can load our slingshots."

"Yeah," Susie said. She held out a big wicked-looking Y-shaped piece of wood with a wide strip of rubber attached to it. "We got lots of slingshots.

94

And lots of rocks. I've been collecting rocks down in the creek. They're piled up over there behind the barricade. See the barricade?"

Ari looked. On the far side of the clearing, at the edge of the trees, an old wooden table had been turned on its side. Susie grabbed his arm and dragged him toward it. Behind the table were several piles of large, mean-looking rocks.

"And here's your slingshot," Susie was saying.

Ari looked at Aurora. She was shaking her head again. "No, Kate," she said. "No slingshots. No rocks. Don't you see? Don't you see that if we shoot rocks at them—something terrible will happen? It will. I know it will."

"Yeah." Kate's voice was tight and angry. "To them it will. Something terrible will happen to those creeps if they think they can—"

She stopped in midsentence. "Listen," she whispered. "I hear them."

Then they all heard them. The PROs were coming across the Weedpatch.

Chapter

15

Carlos had awakened that morning knowing something was wrong before he remembered exactly what it was. For a few seconds before he was entirely awake he lay very still, trying to go back to sleep—so he wouldn't have to remember. But it didn't work.

This was the day the PROs were going to chop down the Dragoland grove to make room for first base. Which would have been great except a bunch of ecology nuts were going to try to stop them. And Bucky was going to show up with baseball bats and a hatchet and *a pellet gun*. And the whole thing had been his, Carlos Garcia's, idea, so whatever happened was going to be his fault. Carlos tried pulling the covers over his head, but it didn't help much, so he gave up and got out of bed.

He was still sitting on the foot of his bed putting on his shoes when he heard his mom calling him from downstairs.

"Carlos," she called. "Bucky's here. Carlos. Can you come right down?" She sounded a little bit frantic, which probably meant Bucky was driving her crazy.

"Coming," Carlos yelled and ran down the stairs with one shoe half on. In the kitchen Carlos's mom was at the grill turning pancakes. The only other Garcia present was Rafe, who was leaning against the sink drinking a glass of orange juice. As usual he was wearing his football practice outfit and a cool, sarcastic grin. Bucky was sitting at the kitchen table scarfing down pancakes.

"Hey, Bro," Rafe said. "You better get going before your buddy here finishes breakfast and starts doing lunch."

Carlos glared at Rafe. "Come on, Bucky," he said. "Let's get out of here."

Bucky stuffed a whole pancake into his mouth and then sprayed pancake crumbs all over the floor as he mumbled something that might have been "thank you." Then he ran out the back door while Carlos was still telling his mom she didn't have to save him any pancakes because he wasn't very hungry.

When Carlos caught up with Bucky he was pulling a huge plastic garbage bag out from under the hedge. Strange, sinister-looking shapes bulged the shiny black surface of the bag. As Bucky swung it up over his shoulder he grinned at Carlos and said, "I bet you can't wait to see what I've got in here."

"I can wait," Carlos said. He was noticing that Bucky's eyes looked blank and fixed and he had the same wild-man grin on his face that usually meant he was headed for a basket and you better get out of his way.

As they were crossing the Castle Court circle Carlos said, "Bucky, I don't think . . ." He pointed to the bag. "I think maybe we oughtn't to . . ." But Bucky wasn't paying attention.

"Eddy will be in the Pit," he said between his grinning teeth. "I called him. He said he'd bring Web too. They're going to wait for us there. Come on. Hurry up."

Eddy and Web were in the Pit, all right, and as soon as they'd all said "hi," Eddy asked where Lump was.

"Oh yeah. Lump," Carlos said. He'd forgotten all about bringing Lump. "I could go back for him," he said.

"Naw, forget it. We won't need him," Bucky said. "Wait till you see what I've got." He untied the top of his sack and began taking stuff out. First he took out two baseball bats and then a shiny, sharp-looking hatchet. He picked up the hatchet, looked at

Carlos for a moment, and then handed it to Eddy. "Here, Eddy. You take this," he said. "You get to have first turn with the hatchet." He handed one bat to Carlos and the other to Web. Then he reached back into the sack and pulled out—a gun.

The gun looked rusty and kind of handmade, but it had a long evil-looking barrel. "Hey, Bucky, we don't need that thing," Carlos said. "Put that back in—"

"It's for the snake," Bucky said. "I told you, it's just for the snake." He looked at Eddy. "You don't want to start chopping trees with a live python in one of them, do you?"

Eddy stared at the gun. His eyes had a strange, glazed look to them. Nodding and shaking his head at the same time, he said, "Yeah, yeah. I don't like live snakes."

"See, Carlos," Bucky said. "We've got to be prepared for anything. Come on, you guys. I'll lead the way." He climbed up out of the Pit, with Eddy and Web following close behind him. "Come on, Garcia," he called back over his shoulder. "Forward march."

As Bucky started across the Weedpatch carrying his pellet gun like an assault rifle, with Eddy and Web stumbling along behind him, Carlos brought up the rear, still trying to get Bucky's attention.

"Bucky," he kept saying, "Bucky, wait a minute. I don't think this . . . I've got this awful feeling . . ." But Bucky just kept on going.

They were getting pretty close to the grove by then and—nothing was happening. *Maybe*, Carlos thought, with a great rush of relief, *there's not going to be anyone there.*

But then Bucky stopped and Eddy and Web ran into him and Carlos almost ran into them.

"Look," Bucky said. "I just saw a face. Right over there in that bunch of bamboo."

While the three PROs and Web were walking across the Weedpatch, a lot was happening inside the grove. Kate was doing most of it. First she grabbed Aurora and Carson and dragged them back behind the overturned picnic table. Ari followed.

"Yeah," Kate said. "You too, Ari. All of you. You crouch down right there behind the barricade and get your slingshots ready. You too, Susie."

"No." Susie was jumping up and down looking like a fierce, wild-eyed baby rabbit. "No. Not me. I'm going with you. I'm going to go with you, Kate."

"Well, okay, but be quiet," Kate said. "I'm just going to go look out the spy hole."

"Yeah, yeah, me too," Susie said.

Kate stepped carefully over the booby-trap string and disappeared, with Susie right on her heels. Ari stood up for a moment to watch them go and then crouched back down behind the barricade between Aurora and Carson. Aurora had dropped her slingshot and was sitting perfectly still. Carson had a rock in his sling and was trying to aim it, but the wide rubber band was stronger than he was. Every time he pulled on the rock the slingshot tipped over backward. Ari decided to try his.

Even though Ari was stronger than Carson he didn't have much better luck. Every time he had his slingshot almost aimed his bulletproof vest got in his way. A phone book might be a good bullet stopper but it sure was big, not to mention heavy. The shoestrings were beginning to hurt the back of his neck. He was still trying to adjust his vest when Kate and Susie came running back into the clearing. Kate's eyes were wide and excited.

"Get ready," she said as she ducked down behind the barricade. "Get ready. Here they come."

Crouched behind the picnic table, Ari could hear feet tromping and leaves rustling. He heard the stomping get louder—and then, suddenly, a startling metallic clatter. Kate giggled wildly. "The booby trap," she said. "Get ready."

Ari was watching Kate loading her slingshot and

trying to do exactly as she did, when suddenly everything got quiet. A strange deadly quiet. No rustles, no voices, no tin-can clatter. Out of the corner of his eye Ari saw Kate getting to her feet so he did too—and found himself face to face with Bucky Brockhurst and Eddy and Web Wong, and behind them, Carlos Garcia. Eddy was holding a hatchet and Web had a baseball bat. Bucky had a gun—and the gun was pointing right at Kate Nicely. And Kate's slingshot was aimed right at Bucky.

For one terrible moment Ari stared from Kate to Bucky and back again. He wanted to scream at them. To yell, "No! Stop! Don't do it!" but his voice seemed stuck in his throat. But then just as Kate started to pull the slingshot strap farther back there was a sudden thudding noise, a howl of pain, and, right by Ari's feet, Carson Nicely flopped over backward, holding his head. Kate dropped her slingshot and crouched down beside her brother.

"What is it?" she said. "What happened, Carson? Are you shot?"

Carson stopped howling and rubbed his head. "That stupid slingshot," he said. He picked it up and held it out to her. "See. My hand slipped and the handle came back and hit me. Owww!"

Ari couldn't help grinning. Holding up his own slingshot, he tried to see how clumsy old Carson had managed to shoot himself in the head with the handle. He was pulling back on the strap, trying it out, when he glanced across the barricade—and froze with horror.

Although Eddy and Web had moved closer to peek over the barricade and see what had happened to Carson, Bucky hadn't moved an inch. He was still standing right there in the middle of the clearing and he was still aiming his gun. Only now it was pointing right at Ari's head.

Ari gasped, dropped his slingshot, and tried to lift his bulletproof vest up in front of his face. But the shoestrings were tied too tightly. "Wait a minute," he yelled at Bucky. "Wait a minute."

He was still frantically tugging on the phone book when he realized that someone else was standing up behind the barricade. It was Aurora. One hand was pressed against her mouth and the other was raised in the air.

"Hush," she said. "Be still. Listen." And there was something in her face and voice that made everyone in the clearing do exactly what she said.

And then in the quiet that followed, they all heard it—the sound of screaming. They all stood perfectly still while the desperate, frantic sound came closer and closer.

Chapter

16

As the sound of screaming got louder and clearer Aurora suddenly pushed past Ari and ran out from behind the barricade. Ari watched in amazement as his sister seemed almost to fly across the clearing, her huge mop of hair streaming behind her like a curly cape. Darting between Bucky and Web, she pushed Carlos Garcia out of her way and went on running.

"Aurora?" Carlos called after her. "What is it? Who's screaming?"

"Athena," Aurora called back as she disappeared into the bamboo thicket. "It's Athena."

"Athena," Ari said in a strange, high-pitched voice that he hardly recognized as his own. Aurora had known it was their little sister who was screaming, but he hadn't. He didn't know why he hadn't known, except that he had never before heard Athena make a terrible noise like that. Jerking his bulletproof vest over his head, he threw it on the ground and ran after Aurora.

When Aurora and Ari reached the Weedpatch there was no one in sight, but the screaming, gasping, shrieking sound was very near. And then there she was, scrambling up over the back wall of the Pit. Staggering to her feet, Athena ran toward them, her mouth wide open and her face red and wet with tears. When she reached them she threw herself into Aurora's arms.

"What is it?" Aurora said. "What happened? Athena, what happened to you?" But for what seemed like a very long time Athena would only cling to Aurora and wail. While she was still howling Kate arrived and then, close behind her, all the rest of them. Susie and Carson first, and then right behind them all of the guys on the other side.

Bucky and Carlos and Eddy and Web were all there, crowded around Aurora and Athena. But their weapons weren't. No slingshots or hatchets or bats—and no pellet gun either. They must have forgotten all that stuff, Ari thought, somewhere back in the grove. And now everyone, both sides of the war, was standing in a circle, watching Athena as she went on screaming at the top of her lungs.

"What is it?" Aurora kept saying and finally

Athena raised her wet, red-eyed face and gasped, choked, gasped again, and wailed, "It's Prince. It's Prince, Aurora. Prince is dead." Then she buried her face in Aurora's hair and went on sobbing.

"Prince?" Ari gasped. He stopped for a moment as the meaning of the words began to sink in. "Prince is—dead?"

"Yeah," Carlos said in a strange, hushed voice. "The old pony. The old pony finally died."

"Wow," Bucky said. "A dead horse. You ever see a whole dead horse before, Eddy?"

Eddy shook his head.

"Me neither," Bucky said. "Come on. Let's go look."

Bucky started off with Eddy close behind him. No one else moved or spoke for a few seconds but then Carson and Web looked at each other. They didn't say anything—but after a while Carson nodded, Web nodded back, and they started off toward the Andersons' pasture.

After Carlos watched the other PROs go he turned back—and noticed his little sister for the first time. "Susie," he said in amazement.

"Yeah," Susie said. She put her hands on her hips and glared at her brother and he stared back.

After a while he said, "Yeah, well it figures, I

guess. That was you on the phone, wasn't it? That's how they knew everything we were going to do."

Susie stuck out her chin. "Yeah," she said. "I was mad at you. I was mad 'cause you ate up all my birthday present Dove bars."

"Yeah?" Carlos asked. "I guess I forgot they were yours." He stared at Susie for another few seconds. "Hey," he said. "We better go. I haven't eaten breakfast yet. Have you?"

Susie nodded. "Yep," she said. "A long time ago. But I want to go too. I want to see Prince."

So Carlos and Susie left and Ari decided to go with them. At the edge of the Pit he turned to look back and saw that Kate and Aurora were coming too. Kate was carrying Athena.

Kate carried Athena all the way through Dragoland and across the circle. Even though she was unusually tiny for a four-year-old she was getting pretty heavy by the time they got to the Andersons' pasture. But when Kate tried to put her down she only tightened her arms around Kate's neck and hung on fiercely.

Everyone else was already there. All the kids who had just been in the war were there, along with three Anderson grandkids and even old Mr. A. himself. The two littlest grandkids were wiping their eyes and sniffing and Mr. A. had his arms around their shoulders. And there, stretched out on his side in the middle of the circle, was the old pony.

Kate had seen Prince lying down before but this was different. This time his legs stuck out stiffly, his lips were pulled back from his old yellow teeth, and his eyes seemed sunken into his head. There was no doubt about it. Athena was right. Prince was dead.

Kate looked around. Everyone was staring silently. Kate knew how they were feeling because she felt it too. There was something so terrible, so solemn and final about the old horse lying there so stiff and dead, when only the day before he had been standing at the fence like always, waiting for somebody to visit him. And the somebody had usually been Athena.

As if in answer to her thoughts Athena suddenly raised her head from Kate's shoulder, glanced at Prince, and began to wail more loudly than ever. As she screamed she began to thrash around, waving her arms and kicking with both legs. Kate put her down on the ground. Both Kate and Aurora were bending over her when a deep voice said, "Here, let me, girls. Let me talk to her."

It was Mr. A. He bent over Athena, lifted her in

his arms, still kicking and thrashing, and walked across the pasture. When he got to the fence he turned and came back again. All the way over and back he talked and talked. Kate couldn't hear what he was saying but she could see his mouth moving, and after a while she could see that Athena had stopped wailing and kicking. After their second trip across the pasture Mr. A. stopped walking and Athena slid down out of his arms. She looked up at him and slowly nodded. Then she pushed back her tangled hair, wiped her face with both hands, and walked back to stand between Aurora and Kate.

Everyone was watching Athena as she came back to the circle around Prince. They watched her reach up and take Aurora's hand and then turn toward Prince. She stared at the dead pony for a long time. After a while she sighed deeply and wiped her eyes again with her free hand. Then she looked up at her sister.

"It's—it's all right, Aurora," she said. "Prince was very old and sick and achy, and now he's gone to where he'll never be sick or achy again. Mr. A. says Prince is happy now."

Everyone looked at Mr. A. "That's right," he said. "Prince lived a long, happy life but lately the poor old fellow's been having a hard time just getting around. I think we should all be glad for Prince and celebrate his long, happy life, instead of crying for him."

Everyone nodded and then Ari Pappas asked, "What kind of celebration, Mr. A.? Are we going to have a big funeral?" Ari was always asking questions. Before Mr. A. could even answer, Ari asked another. "What are you going to do with him? I mean, you know . . ." Ari motioned toward where the pony was lying. "You know, with—the body?"

"I guess I'll have to call the humane society," Mr. A. said. "They have a truck they send out to pick up dead animals."

"Where will they take him?" Ari asked. "I mean, is there a cemetery for dead ponies?"

Before Mr. A. could answer, Bucky Brockhurst broke in. "Naw," he said. "They'll just take him to the dog food factory. That's what they do with dead horses. They just chop them up and make dog meat out of them."

Athena gasped. She stared at Bucky and then at Prince. Then she threw herself on the ground and started to scream louder than ever.

Chapter

17

At four o'clock that afternoon Ari Pappas sat on the fence at one end of Prince's pasture and wrote in his notebook. He had a lot to write about. He wanted to get the whole thing down from beginning to end—especially the part about what Mr. A. had done when Bucky Brockhurst shot off his mouth about Prince going to the dog food factory.

What Mr. A. had done was to pick Bucky up by the back of his camouflage jacket and shake him. And while he was shaking he was saying something about "somebody else getting turned into dog meat if he didn't keep his big mouth shut."

Then Mr. A. went off toward his house and was gone for quite a long time. While he was gone Ari scooted home and got his fanny pack. So when Mr. A. came back driving his tractor, Ari was ready to get down in writing all the exciting stuff that happened next. He turned past the beginning of "The Diamond War" story and wrote a new title at the tope of the next page. The title of the new story was "The Sad Death of Prince of Castle Court."

What happened next was that Mr. A. explained to everyone how he had called his friend at the humane society and found out that in Castle Court's district you could bury your horse if you wanted to —if you owned at least five acres of land, and if you made the hole nice and deep. So that was why Mr. A. came back in his old tractor with the backhoe attachment all hooked up and ready to go.

Then after he'd picked out a spot right near the middle of the pasture Mr. A. started up the backhoe and began to dig. It was all very interesting. Everybody stood around and watched the hole get deeper, and because the tractor made so much noise other people started coming to watch too.

Rafe and Gabe Garcia, Carlos's big brothers, came first, and then the whole Grant family and their dog, Nijinsky, and Mrs. Anderson with two more grandkids. Mr. and Mrs. Wong and Mrs. Garcia showed up next and after a while Ari's father came too, still wearing his beat-up old metal sculpturing outfit and with his welding goggles perched on top of his head.

At first the new people just stood around explaining what was going on to the newer people, but after a while most of them got put to work. That happened when the backhoe couldn't dig any deeper—and there was still a long way to go to make the grave as deep as the humane society said it had to be. That was when lots of people went home to get shovels and pickaxes and buckets, and Mr. A. sent some grandkids home for a ladder for climbing in and out of the grave.

It took a long time. At noon most of the women went home and got sandwiches and stuff to drink, and the Garcias brought some yard furniture for people to sit on when it wasn't their turn to be down in the hole. Rafe and Gabe and Mr. A. and Mr. Wong and Mr. Grant and Ari's dad did most of the digging, and most of the kids took turns emptying the pails of dirt. Ari would have emptied pails too, if he hadn't had so much to write about.

The last page of Ari's story went like this:

Ladies and gentlemen. I wish you could all be here to see what is happening now. Right this minute they are putting Prince into his grave. Mr. A. and Mr. Wong and Rafe Garcia and my dad each have a hold of one of his legs and they are pulling him toward the edge.

Oh yes. Athena isn't here right now. Aurora

sent her on an errand so she wouldn't have to watch this part of it.

There he goes. Flop. Right down into the hole. And now here comes Athena back again —just in time. Everybody is watching Athena climbing back over the fence with a big carrot in her hand. And now Mrs. A. has starting singing. Mrs. A. is singing "Auld Lang Syne" and everyone is joining in. Everyone is singing "Auld Lang Syne" and Athena is dropping the carrot down into the grave. And now the singing is over and everybody is taking turns hugging Athena, like she was the next of kin, or something. It's kind of weird, actually, but it sure has cheered her up a lot. And all the people who aren't busy hugging Athena are shoveling the dirt back into the hole.

Well, it's over, ladies and gentlemen. Nearly everybody has gone home. The big story of "The Sad Death of Prince of Castle Court" has ended.

Chapter

18

Ari wrote "THE END" in big capital letters and started to close his notebook. But while he was flipping over pages he just happened to notice the other story in the book. The unfinished one called "The Diamond War." He shuddered, thinking about slingshots and pellet guns. There was no telling *when* that horror story would be over.

He finished putting his notebook and pencil away in his fanny pack, climbed down off the fence, and walked over to where Carlos Garcia and Eddy Wong were still shoveling some loose dirt up onto the top of the grave. Nearly everyone had gone home. But Bucky Brockhurst was still watching from one side of the little mound that Carlos and Eddy had made. And on the other side there were just three people, Kate and Aurora and Athena.

When Carlos and Eddy stopped shoveling, Athena climbed up onto the little mound and started smoothing it down with her hands.

"Come on, Athena," Aurora was saying as Ari came up. "Let's go home. Prince's funeral is all over."

Athena shook her head. "No," she said. "I want to stay to see the tombstone. Mr. A. told me he was going to bring a tombstone." She went on patting and smoothing even though her little bitty hands weren't making much of a difference.

"Use your feet," Eddy said to Athena. "Your feet'll work a lot better." Eddy always liked things to be efficient. He stepped up beside Athena on the mound and started taking lots of little steps, tromping down the clods. Athena tromped too for a few minutes, but then she stopped and started digging where a large round rock was sticking up out of the smoothed-down earth.

"Well, I've seen enough," Bucky said. "Come on, Wong and Garcia. Let's go back to Dragoland. We've got some unfinished business to take care of." Grinning his meanest grin right at Kate Nicely, Bucky began to pretend he was chopping down a tree. "Chop, chop, chop!" he said, looking right at Kate.

If Bucky had been trying to start something, which he probably was, it worked. Kate began to look fierce-eyed and tight around the mouth. Getting into a karate pose, she stuck her face right into

Bucky's and whispered, "Chop, chop, chop your-self, you creep. You're the one who's going to get chopped."

Uh-oh, Ari thought. Just what he'd been afraid of. The Diamond War all over again. His hand was just reaching back for his notebook when someone yelled, "And there's the windup and here comes the pitch."

When Ari turned around, Eddy was standing on top of the mound over Prince's grave. Eddy stretched and kicked and almost tied himself in a knot pretending to pitch the baseball-shaped rock that he and Athena had just dug out of the mound.

"Yeah." Carlos was grinning. "It does look sort of like a pitcher's mound, doesn't it?"

"Yeah." Bucky suddenly seemed to forget about yelling in Kate's face. "It sure does." The three PROs stared at each other and then slowly turned to look at what was all around them. At the big open flat field where Prince had lived for so many years. Then, at the same moment, all three of them started running toward Mr. A., who was just coming back into the pasture carrying a big flat board under one arm.

From across the field Ari, Kate, Aurora, and Athena watched while the three PROs jabbered with Mr. A. At first they all seemed to be talking at once, but after a while Bucky and Eddy shut up and let Carlos do most of the talking. And then Mr. A. was nodding his head and the PROs were jumping up and down and yelling and pounding each other on the back. After they'd jumped up and down for a while they took off running toward Carlos's house.

Mr. A. watched them go for a moment before he came on across the field to where Ari and the others were waiting. Mr. A. was grinning. "Well," he said, "I guess this pasture is going to be a baseball diamond, at least for a while." He looked around. "Ought to be okay," he said. "Plenty of room and nothing around here they can break with a fly ball."

Athena tugged at Mr. A.'s sleeve. "But Prince's grave," she said. "And his tombstone. Isn't there going to be a tombstone for Prince?"

Mr. A. squatted down in front of Athena and showed her the big flat board he had in his hands. "Yes, there is, honey," he said. "See this board? I'm going to nail it up on the fence post over there by the street. And I'm going to write 'Prince Field' on it in big letters. And every time there's a big important game we're all going to sing a song to Prince to remind everyone whose field this really is. Won't that be okay?"

Athena tipped her head to one side and thought

for a minute. Then she smiled and nodded. "I guess that's okay," she said. "I think Prince will like that."

A few minutes later Ari and Aurora and Kate were on their way back down the sidewalk. Athena had run on ahead because she saw Nijinsky sitting on his front lawn with his tug-of-war rope in his mouth.

All of a sudden Kate said, "See, you were right. I knew you'd be."

"About what?" Aurora said. But then suddenly her eyes widened. "Yes," she whispered. "It was right. That *feeling* was right. About how Athena was going to be the one to save the Unicorn's Grove."

They stared at each other for a moment longer and then they turned and began to run. Back toward Dragoland and the Unicorn's Grove.

Ari went on alone toward home. He was anxious to get to his room, where he could sit down and write the very last chapter of "The Diamond War."